# EIGHT

# IN

# D

www.BarbarianSpy.com

This book is copyright © habu 2014
habu asserts his right to be known as the author of this work.
Published by BarbarianSpy in 2014
Cover design © S Bush 2014
Cover image: Manipulated: Copyright: FXQuadro at Shutterstock
Ebook ISBN: 978-1-925190-21-2
Paperback ISBN: 978-1-925190-22-9
All rights reserved

BarbarianSpy
Jindalee St
Toronto, NSW 2283
AUSTRALIA

# EIGHT IN D

by

# HABU

# TABLE OF CONTENTS

# INTRODUCTION

The only common thread in this mostly never-before-published collection of eight stories, other than that they are all gay male and that they came from habu's wide-ranging, creative imagination, is that their titles consist of one word, beginning with the letter *D*.

In theme, the stories range from nostalgia to humor to intrigue and deception. The geographic setting for all, except one played out between India and Thailand, is the United States. The stateside locales of this collection are concentrated primarily in and within 100 miles of Washington, D.C., but they also extend from the mid-Atlantic down to Charleston, South Carolina, and out to Mesa Verde, in Arizona. The age of the characters seeking connection ranges from elderly down to barely legal, and most hook-ups are of the older-younger variety.

The opening story, "Debatables," takes us to an exclusive mountain resort in Virginia for a nostalgic, liquor-lathered reunion of a group of men whose past was quite a bit different from their present. "Deceit" is also a nostalgia piece in which a company owner, tired of fighting a corporate takeover, retreats to his gay younger days in Charleston. The layers of subterfuge in "Decoy" play out mostly at a Washington, D.C., professional men's tennis tournament. "Delivery" is one of habu's signature theme stories on the sexual machinations and longings inside a highly—and dangerously--competitive intelligence operation. "Dessert" is a bit of humor on the chores and after-dinner sweets of a boy toy on a visit to Mesa Verde. A young political campaign worker loses his obsessive illusion in "Disillusion." In the only non-U.S. setting story in this collection, the stranded professional escort in "Doublers" finds himself being flown from Mumbai to Bangkok for a double penetration tryst. The concluding story, "Dreamworld," catalogs the transition of an insatiable young man from the world of reality into fantasy.

# Debatables

It was like there was some sort of invincible band of fifteen feet surrounding the group of three who were sitting, looking somewhat bleary eyed, at a table in the center of the smoky bikers' bar on the edge of the town of Hot Springs. It wasn't the table that provided the isolation, because Paul and Thomas had been given the same wide berth when they had been at one of the pool tables. There had been four of them earlier, with three of them having come in a raucous mood, insistent on having a good and very-well-lubricated time. David Eagleton had gotten his fill early, though, and hadn't stayed around for the pool session—followed by several more rounds of drinks.

The bikers still in the bar at 2:00 a.m. weren't being hostile to this alien party of men who obviously had descended on them from the fancy and very expensive Homestead resort hotel up on the hill above the small Virginia mountain town. Nor were they angered that the men were older than most others in the bar, three of them being in their mid-fifties and the fourth a good twenty years older than that. The aliens were putting the liquor away well, except for the older guy, who was more a sipper and watcher. But he too accepted the drinks that were offered

9

to him, which amazed some of the bikers, although it shouldn't have.

It was more that the bikers were bewildered. None of them could remember ever having seen a man in here in a clerical collar before—and putting beers away hand over fist—let alone accompanied by a second, older man in a dress—in a black cassock, also with clerical collar, to be more exact. Few of the bikers could imagine that an old Jesuit priest could be a boozer. But that was just because none of them had actually come in contact with a Jesuit priest before.

Somewhat pie-eyed and holding a scotch bottle by the neck, the younger priest stopped in the middle of a monologue on pranks played on campus over thirty years earlier and looked around at his companions.

"Somebody check the can to see if David's fallen in?" the younger cleric asked in a slurred voice.

"David left hours ago—before you went off to play pool, Brother Thomas," the silken, well-modulated voice of the older man, Monsignor Scarlotti, quietly responded. He leaned over and touched the younger cleric's arm and added, "Perhaps it's time to go back to the hotel. The Debatables aren't on stage until the afternoon tomorrow—or, rather, today—but I have other rounds to put through in the morning."

"I think David was worried about his wife," the third man, Paul Frasier, mumbled. He hiccupped and continued. "Young blonde like that. He probably is worried about her a lot. But if it's because of Chris, I could have told him . . ." His voice trailed off.

"Worried about your Chris, Paul?" Brother Thomas asked, suddenly a bit more sober and with an amused lilt to his voice. "I doubt that's . . ." But his voice too trailed off and he gave a little laugh.

"Drink up; last calls, children," Monsignor Scarlotti said. "It's time we be hanging the reminiscing up and facing life as it is."

There was a long sigh of relief and an atmosphere of comfort drifted into the bar as the three men rose, two of them quite unsteadily, from their chairs, and headed for the exit. The monsignor, although two decades older than the other men, seemed the strongest of the group, even despite the uneven distribution of the liquor. He was the tallest, standing ramrod straight, and thinnest—still with handsome Mediterranean features and a full head of steel-gray hair after all his years as a priest. Despite the austere black cassock, Scarlotti was fully masculine, fully in control.

The other two, younger, but still in their mid-fifties, were a more comical pair, hanging onto each other for dear life as the monsignor guided them out into the night. It's not that they weren't good looking. On the contrary, both were very well put together. But the other cleric, Brother Thomas, was short and thin, with almost feminine features. His hair was still blond, curly, almost falling in ringlets around his head, with just enough silver running through it to make it sparkle in the light. And his facile features were more beautiful—thick, pouting lips and startling pale-blue eyes—than handsome. The other man, Paul Frasier, a very successful TV actor, was stereotyped in mobster-type roles. He was large and hulky—not exactly fat, but thick—and was bald as a billiard cue. His black eyebrows were bushy, and when he set them in an intense look, the TV viewer quickly registered "bad boy trouble." None of this denied that he was ruggedly handsome—perhaps more so at fifty-four than he had ever been earlier in his life.

From somewhere in his flowing cassock, the monsignor, ever in control, produced a flashlight, as he preceded his two charges—young college men again in their imaginations—through the short main street of the sleeping

Hot Springs toward the winding drive up to the Homestead hotel. Those of the village who were still awake smiled as the small procession passed, though. The song the two friends, hanging on to each other for dear life, were singing was in perfect harmony—Brother Thomas' tenor lilting over the steady baritone of Paul Frasier. It was a ribald drinking song that could only amuse when combined with seeing the clerical garb of one of its singers.

\* \* \* \*

"If the subject is abortion, we'll have Amvey— excuse me, Brother Thomas; I understand that you lose the last name when you put on the throat choker—handle the pro argument."

"And if it's corruption in government, you can do the pro honors, Brother David," Brother Thomas countered David Eagleton's little joke.

They were in the Jefferson bar at the Homestead Hotel doing their preliminary drinking earlier in the evening before the Debatables went out carousing in the village at the bottom of the hill. It was an expanded group, minus, for the moment, the monsignor, who was gliding around the hotel's public areas checking on his various teams for tomorrow's events. The three team members, David Eagleton, Paul Frasier, and Brother Thomas, were there, but also huddled around the cocktail table were David's young wife, Amber, and the actor Paul's personal assistant, Chris Cahill.

Amber and Chris, who were lost in a conversation on art while the three Debatables discussed strategy for the next day, were younger than the three mid-fifties team members—by some thirty years each. Amber's husband, David, was studiously not noticing that the two younger people beside him at the cocktail table were getting along famously. Amber was his third wife, a striking blonde, so David had reason ever to be aware of her moods and interests. He was insistent on getting it right this time, even if his circumstances were peculiar, including his life in the public fishbowl. For his part, Chris' employer, Paul, was visibly a bit more concerned that the young people were drifting away from the main discussion.

What the three Debatables had in common was that they were all 1981 graduates of Georgetown University in Washington, D.C., a prestigious university founded by the Jesuits, and that they had constituted the schools collegiate debating team from 1979 to 1981. They were at the ritzy Virginia mountain resort, the Homestead, this weekend, because the university faculty sponsor of all of the school's debating teams from 1980 to the present, Monsignor Scarlotti, had developed a debate extravaganza around its premier team of 1980, the team that had won the national championship that year.

Over the weekend the teams of 1980, 1990, 2000, and 2010 would compete against each other in debates on topics of Monsignor Scarlotti's choosing. The Debatables— that having been the name they had chosen for themselves—were the centerpiece team in this program not only because they had won a national championship but also because of what two of them had become. Paul Frasier was a well-known actor of television and (minor) movies, and David Eagleton was the U.S. congressman for New York's nineteenth congressional district. For his part, Brother Thomas was important as the glue for the entire program. He had become a Jesuit priest and remained at Georgetown, under Monsignor Scarlotti's supervision, and, as an English professor, had trained and sponsored all of the school's debate teams since 1989.

"As the monsignor has selected the topics, though," Brother Thomas continued, "I seriously doubt he would select abortion—and he worked so hard to get David, here, to attend this program that I'm sure he wouldn't include a topic that might embarrass him. I would imagine that at this point in time any political topic would embarrass a sitting U.S. congressmen."

There was a smattering of friendly laughter around the table. The three men had been good-naturedly jabbing at each other all evening with witticisms that came naturally to them."That's debatable," Paul Frasier chimed in. "Scarlotti has a surprising streak in him."

"Monsignor Scarlotti? That stick in the mud? I don't think he'd do anything at all unseemly." This from David.

Paul and Brother Thomas stole a guarded glance at each other and then both gave a little jerk at what they'd done. Thomas recovered quickly. "Debatable. Did I hear you say 'debatable,' Paul?"

And then all three of the old team members laughed, the use of this word having been one they'd overused and laughed about in "the day."

The shared laugh of old times made David catch his breath, though, as he looked over at his wife talking to Paul's personal assistant as if the three older men weren't even there. Thomas' smile as he had laughed and now Chris Cahill's smile as he leaned into Amber to hear what she had to say struck David by the familiarity it emphasized in the two men, albeit decades apart. Paul's personal assistant today was the near double in appearance and almost feminine, sensual blond beauty that Thomas had been back in 1980. How strange, David thought. And neither one of his friends had appeared to notice that.

"What are you two talking about so seriously, sweetheart?" he leaned over to Amber and asked.

"Chris here is an artist too," she answered. "You know how I was telling you that it's so beautiful in the hills around the hotel that I was sorry I hadn't brought my acrylics? Well, Chris brought his. We were discussing the technique of rendering the light of various times of day in landscapes."

"Interesting," David responded, obviously not finding it the least bit interesting. But if Amber was interested in it, he would pretend to keep up. They both did pretense very well.

"We thought that we'd go out and try the late morning light tomorrow," Chris said, turning a young Brother Thomas smile on the New York politician. "We'd be sure to be back for your team's debate tomorrow evening, though," he continued.

"By all means you must catch the late morning light," David responded. He returned the smile, but other emotions were at work as he watched the two younger people talking so enthusiastically about art. The glories of art had escaped him in life, he was afraid.

Amber was looking up at a handsome young waiter who had been very attentive to her all evening and who had brought her a refill of her Margarita nearly as soon as she'd finished the first one. The two exchanged smiles as she handed the empty glass and a napkin back to him.

Amber was fast to flirt with handsome young men, David thought. He wondered how long he'd be able to hold her—although so far their unusual arrangement had held.

"Hold back a bit on the liquor, I would think, young men. It wouldn't do for our best and brightest to be too dull on the morrow."

The five people huddled around the cocktail table looked up to see that the ancient, but well-preserved, prelate who had brought them all here was approaching in a swirl of the folds of the black cassock he had continued to wear long after the Vatican had given dispensation to go more modern. On him, though, the cassock looked good.

He was still thin, strong, and upright as steel after all these decades.

After pleasantries were exchanged all round, Amber excused herself, saying she knew the Debatables weren't close to turning in but that she was weary. In her wake, Chris also excused himself to go to the men's room—"And then, after checking for telegrams at reception, on to my room as well, I think," he said. "There's still a lot of Paul's work needing done in TV land this weekend."

All four men watched the younger, beautiful woman and man move off, separately, toward the hotel lobby, each of the older men thinking his own thoughts of the beauty of them and of a lost youth.

"Well, I'm for exploring the village below," declared Paul, standing.

"It's nearly midnight, Paul," Brother Thomas said, with a small laugh. "Everything will be closed in town."

"That's debatable," Paul answered, and there was a memory-dredging laugh all around. "I'm sure something will be open. Are we too old to get blotto as we always did at school the night before the debate? Have we forgotten how that sharpened our wits? Who's with me?"

"If you put it that way, how could I not rise to the challenge," Brother Thomas said.

"And I too, I guess," David said, coming to his feet. "After I visit the john first, of course. There are some aspects of aging a man simply can't escape."

As David walked off to find the men's room, Monsignor Scarlotti chimed in in a false morose voice, "I suppose I must accompany you to make sure that my prize guests don't get lost in the mountains."

As the group moved toward the lobby, the waiter started picking up empty glasses and wadded napkins. He was in a bit of a hurry, and he was humming.

"What are those over there?"

"The stables, I think. The path up to the hotel is this way, though. Tom. Tom . . ."

Brother Thomas had veered off the path toward the hotel's stables. Paul had moved a few steps in that direction, but he stopped, unsure of going beyond the circle of light shown from the monsignor's flashlight. Monsignor Scarlotti was a couple of steps beyond the two inebriated friends who had been stumbling up the hill supporting each other, but he stopped and turned back when he heard Paul calling for Tom.

"Tom . . . Tom," Paul called out again.

"Tom tom, beat the little drummer boy," Tom's voice rang out. "I want to see the horses. We don't have nearly enough horses in Georgetown." The voice was coming from a bit of a distance away—uphill toward where Paul could see the line of outbuildings against the moonlit skyline.

"I suppose we must indulge him," Monsignor Scarlotti said, as he passed Paul, following in the direction in which Brother Thomas had gone.

Paul and the monsignor hadn't gone far, though, before they heard a clatter, a yelp, and an expletive. When they came upon Brother Thomas, who was sitting on the path and holding his ankle, they could see that he had found not only the stables but also a pile of rakes and hoes.

"You OK, Tom?" Paul asked, bending down beside his friend.

"It's my ankle, I think."

"Can you put any weight on it?"

"In his present state, I don't think he should even try," the monsignor said brusquely. "You'd better help him into the stables and settle him comfortably, and I'll go on up to the hotel for a first aid kit and a crutch. A resort specializing in outdoor activities for the lazy rich certainly should have a store of crutches about."

When the monsignor had departed, Paul put his arms around Brother Thomas and started to raise him up.

"Don't bother, I can walk fine," Brother Thomas murmured. "I just wanted to be alone with you for a while."

"Alone with—?"

"Don't talk, Paul. It's been too long." Paul still had his arms around Brother Thomas, and the cleric pulled him further into the clutch and took Paul's lips in his. The two were transported down the years into memories of their relationship at the university.

"Oh, god," Paul croaked. "I've been hard for you all evening. I thought you had forgotten."

"Never," Brother Thomas whispered. "I want you. I can't wait until we can work something out up at the hotel."

"Why do we have to wait until we're up at the hotel?" Paul murmured. Still strong after all these years and the larger of the two, Paul scooped the cleric up from the ground and carried him into the stables. Nearly half of the stalls were empty, and there were bales of hay about, so it took no time at all for Paul to find a stall and lower Brother Thomas' belly on a hay bale. With the cleric's insistence for speed, Paul quickly had the cleric's trousers and briefs around the other man's ankles and was tonguing and fingering his ass open.

"Just like old times," Brother Thomas moaned as Paul hovered over his back, positioned his cock—which indeed had been hard for Brother Thomas all evening—and started working his way into the anal passage.

They both panted and emitted uncontrolled animal sounds as Paul thrust with his cock and Brother Thomas thrust back with his buttocks and the horses in the stalls nearby moved restlessly against their stall walls, disturbed by the strange noises coming from nearby.

Spent, Paul rolled off Brother Thomas' back and sat, his back against the stall wall beside the hay stack. Brother Thomas, in turn, lowered himself from the hay and sat with his back against the stack and his legs draped over Paul's. Instinctively, each man reached for the cock of the other and they sat there, overlapped, each slowly stroking the other, and both breathing hard. What had been easy thirty years ago no longer was, for either of them. But they both had managed as if it had only been yesterday that they had actively been lovers.

"I had almost forgotten," Paul whispered after his breathing became more controlled.

"I never did," Brother Thomas answered. "You always were the best."

"Don't let the monsignor hear you say that," Paul said with a little laugh. "And he'll be back soon."

"Not too soon," Brother Thomas said. "I timed the walk from the hotel down to here when we went down into the town. We probably have another half hour before he can get back, walking in the dark and having to find a first aid kit. And their medical office is closed at night. They'll have to find someone to open that to get a crutch."

"You mean to say you planned this?"

"Would you be upset with me if I did?" Brother Thomas asked.

"Never."

"The way your personal assistant and David's wife were getting along, I half thought he wouldn't be in the way and we could meet in my room tonight. And maybe we still can if they . . ."

"Chris and David's wife?" Paul said it with a snort. "I hardly think so."

19

"David certainly seemed to think so," Brother Thomas said. "He was nervous and left for the hotel early tonight. He no doubt has his young wife back in line and in his bed by now."

"Oh, you think so? You think David went back for his wife? That's highly debatable. Didn't you see how closely Chris resembles you at that age?"

"I don't know what . . . did you use the word 'debatable' again?"

They both laughed.

"Your assistant, Chris . . ." Brother Thomas now said. "You are fucking him, aren't you?"

"So you noticed," Paul answered.

"That he looks so much like I did back in 1980? Yes. You didn't have to tell me that. When I saw that is when I first believed we might be able to rekindle what we once had."

"And you aren't upset that I kept pursuing the ideal of you beyond the time we spent together?"

"Not in the slightest," Thomas answered in a quiet, hoarse voice.

"We're wasting time, you know," Paul suddenly said. "You said that Scarlotti would be back in about—"

"As you said, we're wasting time," Brother Thomas said, as he came up on his knees and covered Paul's mouth with his.

This time, with Brother Thomas lying on the small of his back on the hay bale, and a trouserless Paul hunched between the smaller man's spread and lifted legs, his ankles held in Paul's fists, the two took a bit too long in the fuck. And they failed to anticipate how silently Monsignor Scarlotti could move in the night.

He was there, inside the stable, watching them, for several minutes before they became aware of his presence. When they did, it was after the monsignor had slowly unbuttoned the thirty-three buttons of his cassock and spread the cassock apart, showing not only that he was naked underneath but also that a firm erection jutted out from his gray pubic bush.

Somewhat shocked, but the scenario being too clear for Paul to bother to try to hide it, Paul turned his head to the monsignor. He didn't seem all that surprised that the priest was naked and erect under his cassock. "You didn't have time to get to the hotel and back—and I don't see a first aid kit. Have you been—?"

"I've been watching from the shadows the entire time, yes," Scarlotti said. "I figured that Brother Thomas would be at you for this. I didn't buy into his charade of a twisting ankle. And you know what I want now."

It was only after the monsignor had saddled up behind Paul and had thrust inside him and was fucking him from behind while Paul was fucking Brother Thomas missionary style that the mentor and his students of thirty years previously were truly traveling back down memory lane.

\* \* \* \*

The three were not exactly missed by those they'd left back at the hotel. David Eagleton, who had carried a crush for Brother Thomas all these years but had suppressed it because Monsignor Scarlotti was in control and Paul Frasier had been there first, had been deeply taken with Chris Cahill earlier in the evening. Chris so closely resembled the young Thomas, who David had pined for but had never won, that David was smitten by him. David followed Chris to the men's room from the Jefferson bar and was delighted to find that Chris had no problem with being propositioned by him. Chris wasn't just Paul Frasier's personal assistant; he also was Paul Frasier's boy toy.

21

While Paul and the clerics were having their memory-lane threesome in the stables, David Eagleton was thoroughly into Chris—in the literal meaning of that word—in Chris' room at the hotel. And David wasn't the least bit worried about where his young wife, Amber, was or what she was doing. They had an arrangement for political reasons.

Amber wasn't being overlooked, however. The message she'd passed to their waiter in the Jefferson bar had had its immediate—and intended—effect. Those two, young, beautiful people were fucking like rabbits in an empty room the waiter had purloined with the help of a friend at the reception desk.

# DECEIT

He had packed a bag before leaving for the pharmaceutical plant out near Christiana Mall that morning. He had a fairly easy commute for Wilmington, Delaware. Whereas most faced heavy traffic coming into the center city, he, with his long-suffering wife, two nonresponsive daughters in college, one lazy dog, and two selfish cats, lived in the exclusive Wawaset community on the western edge of the city. This meant he drove against traffic to get to the plant. His corporate offices were downtown in a high-rise building on North Washington Street, but he had avoided going there for days.

A larger pharmaceutical corporation, Delmarva Pharmaceuticals, had been maneuvering for months to swallow the company that had been in his family for decades, and he just was no longer up to the wrangling his lawyers were putting him through to stem that takeover—at least for today and maybe tomorrow, as well.

Earl Hastings didn't know why he'd packed a bag while his wife was out for her bridge night the evening before and put it in the trunk of his Lexus RC F coup before Muriel had gotten home. Nor could he explain why he'd taken the checking account book and credit cards for the accounts no one else knew about out of the secret compartment in the desk in his study and put them in the glove compartment of the Lexus.

The pressures at the office were more than duplicated at home. His wife was bugging him about the plans for the far-too-ostentatious country home being built for them west of the city in Kennett Square, Pennsylvania. He was having second and third thoughts about leaving the Wawaset house he grew up in but that his wife professed to hate. His daughters were competing with each other for who was going to flunk out of their ultra-expensive university first, and not tell their parents in time to save them, as well as who was going to get pregnant by a swimming coach first. And even the family dog had become incontinent. It was Muriel's dog, or he'd have a care about that.

He just knew he wanted options. If he couldn't have an hour's rest from the lawyers and company strategizers at his office out at the plant, he had an option.

Sometime before lunch that day, Earl Hasting walked out of his office at the plant, got into his Lexus coup, and started driving south. Three days later, after uncomfortable nights in cheap hotels en route, he drove into Charleston, South Carolina, and to a real estate office. By 6:00 p.m. that evening he had signed an immediate occupancy contract for a fully furnished three-story, three-bedroom, two-car garage townhouse in Simonton Mews in the center of Charleston, three blocks south of the King Street main drag.

He had no intention of staying six months. He didn't even know if he would be staying the week. All he knew for sure was that he had to get out of Wilmington and away from everything there, including his family. He didn't even consider a hotel. He wanted to disappear into the wall, to have a garage where he could hide his fancy coup, and he wanted to do foolish things. Renting a house for six months was a foolish thing.

There were other foolish things he'd always dreamed about doing, though—including ones he'd actually done before the staid life heading up a pharmaceuticals company, marrying and raising a family, and attending a church he didn't believe in every Sunday grabbed and emasculated him.

Until day two, when he took a walk around the neighborhood, he didn't even know why he had driven straight to Charleston from Wilmington, or why he had settled on a house in this neighborhood. Walking four blocks south from his house, though, he started seeing buildings he recognized, buildings that calmed him and that had fond memories for him. This is where he'd gone to graduate school—at the College of Pharmacy of the Medical University of South Carolina. This was where he had lived life—for two years—as he wanted to without all of the pretense and sacrifice that went with being destined to take over his family's business.

And why had he leaped at the Simonton Mews house? It was because four blocks in the opposite direction, north, was the Ann Street district. This was where he had met Sandy while he'd been in graduate school. It had been the happiest year of Earl's life. But it was a year he had had to bury and never speak of.

Once Earl had realized why he'd come to Charleston to hide out, it took him two more days to work up the courage to walk over to Ann Street in the evening. Nothing was there that had been there when he'd been a student, but the street was still where one went for what he'd gone for back then. The clubs there now were Club Pantheon and Dudley's. They were just a few doors away from each other. Earl could tell as he walked down the street that he was in the right place. Groups of young men were standing

25

out on the sidewalks, conversing with each other, checking passersby out, smoking their cigarettes and joints, and, some, posing for possibilities when cars cruising down the street slowed down or paused.

Earl was gratified that he still received inviting looks, no doubt, now that he was in his late forties, helped out by the obviously expensive clothing he wore—and how well he wore them. But he had kept the rugged good looks he'd had in his twenties, and he'd kept his trim, but well-muscled physique as well. He'd actively played sports and attended the gym often enough to keep in shape. He was very competitive in both golf and tennis.

He went into Club Pantheon. The music was loud, as was the decibel level of conversation, both blending so that neither was decipherable. And the room was smoky. But the crowd was comforting for Earl. He could move around, become accustomed to a scene he once had indulged in, and call up those sensations that had made him feel electrified and so on edge "back then."

He wondered what had happened to Sandy. He didn't expect to find him here anymore, but he had an image of the young man—still as young now as he was then—in his mind, and he kept looking into the face of every young man he encountered while roaming around the crowded room, where everywhere seemed to be either dance floor or conversation pit or proposition auction, depending on what suited the men interacting at the moment.

He had moved around the room twice before he saw him. Reddish-blond hair, maybe in his mid-twenties, more beautiful than handsome, smiling prettily for an older man who had just handed him a drink where he was perched on a barstool and had leaned in to him. The spitting image of Sandy.

A dark-haired youth, not much more than twenty—small of stature, olive skinned—had been following behind Earl on his second circuit of the room. He caught up with Earl at the moment.

"Hello. I haven't seen you in here before. Are you with anyone?"

Earl focused on the young man. He was quite good looking and a bit saucy. Earl felt himself go harder—he'd already worked up a half-hard just because of the musky odor of men in heat hunting in the room. This lad would do—if the man pressing in on the younger man with the reddish-blond hair, who Earl was already thinking of as Sandy, was staking a claim in that department. Earl glanced back at the bar, where the deal between those two men seemed to have been set. With a sigh, he refocused on the dark-haired young man who had approached him.

"I'm new to town," Earl answered.

The dark-haired young man touched the sleeve of Earl's silk shirt, gave him a come-hither look, and asked in a throaty voice, "Buy a guy a drink? There are great possibilities if you do—and if you're interested."

While they were drinking their scotches—Earl had asked for a good brand so the young man would know he was well-heeled, if Tony, as that was what he'd said his name was, hadn't gathered that already before he had approached Earl—the older man asked if there were other gay-friendly establishments around.

"There's Dudley's up the street," Tony said. "It's not as lively as here, though. And not as much variety. A younger crowd, with more than a smattering of straights. I find it so much more copasetic and stimulating here."

Earl could tell that Tony was using sophisticated words—or trying to—and was striking Bette Davis poses because he was trying to make Earl. There wouldn't be any surprise or indignation or beating around the bush. Earl wanted to tell him he was trying too hard. But then Earl didn't want to start all over with someone else—not unless the red-headed guy became available.

"I meant I wondered if there were any places with rooms for short-term rent in the neighborhood."

"Is that what you're interested in, sugar?"

Tony had suddenly acquired a southern accent. Earl wanted him to shut up and just get on with it. The longer they talked, the less attractive Tony was. But the longer Earl was here the more needy he was.

"Is there a short-term fuck hotel nearby, and what do you charge?"

There was such a hotel, Tony said, a bit startled. And for $100 he gave and received a blow job and let Earl furiously fuck him doggy style on a lumpy mattress with a rocking and squeaky brass bed frame.

After it was over, with Tony genuinely marveling at the size of Earl and his obvious need, Earl realized that this was exactly what he'd left Wilmington for—what he had needed to decompress from the tension and pressure both at work and at home. A week running of this, he decided, and he'd be renewed and ready to face the corporate challenge again. He already was beginning to formulate new strategies in his mind to stave off the grab for his company.

He'd go to Ann Street each night for a week, but he wouldn't take anyone to the Simonton Mews house, and he'd fuck a different young man each night. He'd only repeat if he saw the young man he increasingly identified as Sandy in his mind again and could hook up with him. Than after a week, he'd go home to Wilmington, turn his back for a second time on this lifestyle choice, and give his enemies hell. He'd be invincible.

Earl paid for a room at the fleabag in advance for an hour and half a night for the next week. And he returned to Club Pantheon each night. He continually was on the lookout for Sandy, and he thought from time to time that he'd gotten a glimpse of the young man. But he never got close enough to him to proposition him.

He, in turn, was propositioned at every turn. Word had gotten out that there was a crazy middle-aged sugar daddy with a fat wallet and an equally fat cock who could fuck like a wild man. Each night for the next four nights, he took a different young man to the fleabag hotel and fucked the stuffing out of him. Each night Earl got less inhibited and more forceful with his sex drive. And each succeeding night he drew more attention from the young men at Club Pantheon.

The fifth night, a Friday night, he was approached by Clifford. Clifford Evans wasn't like any of the young men Earl had gone with. He was nearly Earl's own age. And, if anything, he was more expensively and elegantly dressed than Earl was. He approached Earl with confidence and the other men buzzing around Earl backed off as if Clifford was visiting royalty.

It was Clifford who bought the scotches, not Earl— and it was better quality scotch than Earl had ordered.

And it was Clifford who asked what Earl's stud fee would be. Bemused and caught off guard by this entirely different encounter and half thinking this was a joke, Earl named a high price. Clifford accepted it without a blink of an eye. There would be no fleabag hotel room with a creaking bed, though.

Earl fucked Clifford in the back of his limousine as it was driven out into the countryside beyond Charleston. Earl had never been with a mature man before, and he found the greater experience of a man of Clifford's age and sophistication to be exhilarating.

They fucked twice as the limousine glided through the countryside. Between fuckings, while they both smoked cigarettes and regained their breath and erections, Clifford complemented Earl on not only his sexual prowess but also his conditioning. When Earl told him that he played tennis regularly, Clifford said that he did too, and he invited Earl to play a couple of sets with him at his country club the next afternoon.

"I know of a couple of luscious young men who will be there who will be happy to play doubles, if you like. And you can take your pick of them to fuck afterward."

Intrigued, Earl accepted the invitation and gave his Simonton Mews address for a limousine pickup the next day.

* * * *

Earl's first surprise when Clifford's limousine delivered him to the entrance of the Charleston Country Club was that Clifford wasn't a full member. Earl saw when he checked in as Clifford's guest that Clifford was a temporary member. Earl assumed that membership in this club would cost a pretty penny, but he had also assumed that Clifford was a permanent local resident. He had intimated that to Earl, and he certainly knew his way around the city and adjacent countryside—or at least his chauffeur did.

So, Earl thought, Clifford was also here from somewhere else. Of course Earl hadn't given Clifford any reason to think he was hiding out in Charleston from anywhere else. Maybe we both are, Earl thought.

The second surprise came when Clifford guided Earl through the club's bar and out onto the patio overlooking the golf course's 18th hole, with its umbrella-covered patio tables and gaggle of bored rich bitch housewives in golf togs or skimpy tennis dresses. There were two young men sitting at the table Earl was guided to—both young men were known to Earl in differing shades of "known." Tony, the first young man Earl had met at Club Pantheon and bedded at a fleabag hotel nearby was there. But also sitting there on the club's terrace was "Sandy," the young man who had dredged up Earl's misbegotten graduate school days in his mind and who had been elusive on Earl's visits to Club Pantheon.

Clifford brought Earl to a temporary halt when he first caught sight of the young men—and before they saw the two older men had arrived—laid a hand on Earl's forearm and whispered in his ear, "Afterward, you can have either one—either in my limousine or as a takeaway. I've paid for both. Do you know which one you fancy the best?"

Of course Earl did. "The one with the reddish-blond hair."

"Ah, Andy then."

Earl nearly snorted. Andy was so close to Sandy that it must be the devil who was setting this up for him. Earl took a hard look at Clifford, but he was smiling blandly and Earl saw no evidence of horns at his temples.

"In that case, you will partner in tennis with Tony—so that Andy will be across the net from you for you to ogle at your heart's content. If making you inattentive will be an advantage for me in the play, your contemplation of the play afterward will more than compensate, I presume."

Watching Andy across the net was, indeed, distracting for Earl, not the least because when the four men were sitting on the patio, becoming acquainted, Andy made no bones about knowing what came afterward—or showed any displeasure at the prospect. Earl was an expert tennis player, though, and he and Tony won handily anyway.

The men played shirtless, and Earl wouldn't have thrown any of the other three out of bed.

In the men's room afterward, when Clifford asked Earl where he wanted to fuck Andy and Earl asked that Clifford's chauffeur drive Andy and him back to the Simonton Mews house—having completely forgotten all intentions of keeping his home in Charleston separate from his sexual activities—Earl asked Clifford why he was doing this for him.

"It's so hard to find good tennis competition," he said, at first, and then when he saw that it had been a serious question, he said, "You have made me happy, and will, I hope, continue to make me happy. I have seen you ogling those two young men at Club Pantheon. I can afford to cover the happiness of us both."

Earl was so besotted with the prospect of fucking Andy at this point that he didn't pursue the issue further. Clifford had never asked how much Earl was worth—but surely he could see from what Earl wore, the money he had dropped at Club Pantheon before Clifford had entered the scene, and by where he lived that Earl must also be well heeled himself. Clifford made Earl feel like a prostitute—but Earl was still trying to think of reasons why that should bother him. Maybe feeling cheap and used was what he needed.

Such was Earl's exhilaration at having Andy—the symbol of his long-lost lover, Sandy—in his grasp that it was surprising the two did make it to a proper place for fucking the first time. Just inside the door to the Simonton Mews house, Earl drew the smaller, younger man to him into a close embrace, and they kissed deeply. Andy was fully yielding to Earl and even reached between them and rubbed Earl's crotch to inflame the man further.

Pulling away from the kiss, Earl murmured, "We'll get out of these sweaty tennis clothes and shower first. Upstairs."

"Yes," Andy answered, but he pulled Earl in for another kiss, and when he turned to mount the stairs, he wiggled his buttocks as he climbed. It was his buttocks that got mounted right then and there, as Earl rose up the staircase behind Andy, bent him over so that he was standing, spreading his legs on one stair, his cheek was firmly pushed into the carpeted tread five stairs farther up, and he reached up the stairs and clawed at the carpeting on the tread. Earl crouched over him, pulled his tennis shorts down his thighs, pushed a thick, erect phallus around the butt strap of the jock strap, and forced himself inside the younger man.

Andy made all of the sounds of taking a thick cock in a tight channel—and wanting to do so—that inflamed Earl to continue with the assault. Earl thrust again and again, each time managing more depth, each time triggering a call of "Yes, fuck me, hard," from the young man trapped underneath him.

The fuck was frenzied, and they had not taken time for the niceties of a condom. Neither man mentioned that subsequently, though, and after that first animalistic assault, their sex became more regularized and followed a pattern of showering thoroughly, after which Andy sucked Earl's cock until Earl was worked up to do the same for Andy. This was followed by the ritual of Andy crowning Earl's cock with a condom in affirmation and acceptance of what was to come, and then a brief wrestling match on the bed or floor or sofa or table for control, with Earl asserting himself, and then fucking the stuffing out of Andy—in every position they could imagine.

Earl was so besotted with Andy that he fucked him for three days straight, with just brief toilet, meal, and sleep breaks, without either leaving the Simonton Mews house. It wasn't until the morning of the fourth day, over breakfast at the table in the bow window overlooking the treed green space that ran between the fronts of the houses in the mews, that they began to get acquainted on a personal level.

Andy was sitting there, just in a robe, sitting sideways to the table, a bare foot propped up on the rung of the chair beside his and sipping on his coffee, reddish-blond hair ruffled, and looking slightly sleepy. The robe was open to show a shapely calf and thigh and the bulb of his cock peeking out over the curve of his thigh. At no time before this did he remind Earl of Sandy more than this—a Sandy who had not aged; a Sandy who accepted Earl's cock even though time hadn't stood still for Earl, a Sandy who knew just how to pose when he wanted to be fucked by Earl.

The young man spoke of being a student—in music—at the College of Charleston, the campus of which started just three blocks to the east, toward the tip of the historical district projecting into where the Ashley and Cooper rivers merged, separated from the Atlantic Ocean only by Charleston Harbor.

Earl slowly ran a hand up the line of Andy's leg until, reaching the cock head, he was cupping the young man's dick and pressing a thumb into the piss slit of the bulb. Andy sighed and moved his calf over Earl's knee to give Earl all the access he wanted.

"It's the summer break," Andy continued. "I stayed on to continue my piano studies—although the oboe is my favorite instrument. I was playing pickup at Club Pantheon to make ends meet. And then Mr. Evans said he'd pay me to be your companion."

"And that's worth being only with me?"

"It's a pile. It's enough to cover my first semester tuition next year too." But Andy faltered here, suddenly realizing what this meant in terms of his budding relationship to Earl. His ready yielding to Earl wasn't an act. "But I didn't know then how it would be with you," he said, speaking shyly and looking into his cup rather than up into Earl's eyes.

Earl was close beside him, also only in a robe, arms of the two around each other's shoulders, and one of Andy's legs hooked on Earl's knee. Earl was cupping Andy's balls with his free hand and absentmindedly pulling down on them and stroking the young man's stiffening cock with his forefinger. Andy slid down a bit in his chair and moved his leg higher on Earl's thigh, giving Earl access to more than the dick and balls. Earl's forefinger moved below the balls, between the buttocks, searching for and finding the warm depths of the channel. Finding it and entering. Andy groaned and leaned his face into Earl's for a deep kiss. Andy had been open to Earl like this from the start, no inhibitions, no pulling back—whatever Earl wanted to do, wherever he wanted to do it.

Earl was sitting straight on to the large bow window with a view of the leafy green branches beyond. The extended kitchen was on the second floor of the three-story townhouse. An entrance, study and laundry room and a double garage, opening to the rear of the house, was under them.

When they came out of the kiss and Earl's middle finger joined his forefinger in the depths of Andy's ass cleavage and, to sighs from Andy, he began moving them in and out, Earl looked around the kitchen extending into this dining area and then across the stair landing into the living room, seeing the place for the first time, and admiring the furnishings. They were both stylish and comfortable. This was a place he could live—with Andy.

He took his hand from Andy's channel, but only long enough to untie the sash of Andy's robe, to let his chest be exposed, to run his hand up the hard-muscled torso of the young man, stopping briefly at the taut nipples, before returning to playing with his balls and hard dick and moving to his rim.

"No, keep the money. And I'll be happy to provide more for your second semester." He didn't want to say at that moment what that meant to him in terms of their ongoing arrangement, but he assumed Andy would get the gist of it. He had no idea why Clifford would give Andy so much money to do this, but he didn't want to think about that now. He wanted to think back to when he was a graduate student here and living with Sandy—and aching for that arrangement never to end. But it had. He'd come from an entirely different world and he'd gone back to it. It had been his decision, not Sandy's.

Had it been a good decision? If he had it to do all over again, would he have stayed? Could he just stay here now—with Andy? He certainly had enough money set aside that no one in his other world knew about that he could do that now. Would he let this second chance pass him by?

"Fuck me, please fuck me," Andy murmured. He untied Earl's sash, and reached for his cock, which was in full erection.

"Now, later, tomorrow, always," Earl whispered.

"Are you saying I could stay here with you?" Andy asked. Earl turned his face to him. There were tears in his eyes. He didn't really have to say anything for Andy to understand. Thus far Andy hadn't asked anything about Earl's life. But now he did.

"You're not married or anything, are you? No children. I wouldn't be breaking up a family or anything, would I?"

"No, I'm not married—and I don't have any children." The deceit readily came out of Earl's mouth, but of course this changed everything. This shattered his new world. He could continue with Andy, but now it would be a relationship built on deception. Would that eat away at him? Would it make him constantly think about the responsibilities and obligations he'd walked away from in Delaware? He had been telling himself that it was only a breather, a way to regroup so that he could come back even stronger in fighting Delmarva Pharmaceuticals for control of his company and for arming him better to face his problems with his family objectively and without bitterness.

Would the deception he had just committed change everything? He didn't want to think about it now.

"I think I'd like to go upstairs, now," he said huskily.

There were many things Andy could have done at that point. He could have said he wasn't finished with his breakfast. Indeed, his plate wasn't clean and his coffee cup wasn't empty. Or he could have used the occasion to wheedle more privilege or leverage from the middle-aged man across the table from him. Or he could have whined about just being Earl's sex toy. But what he did—which made him so much like Sandy and which mentally transported Earl back to the days he remembered as so much happier than any time since—was to give Earl a radiant smile.

"Why not right here?"

"Why indeed not?" Earl answered with a throaty laugh "Both here and upstairs. Sit on it."

Andy rose from his chair, straddled Earl's thighs, and reached back to Earl's cock, steady and upright, so that he could descend on it. Earl reached over to the tabletop to retrieve one of the many condom packets he kept around the house.

Later, Andy was lying on his back at the foot of the bed, his legs spread and bent, his heels pressed into the edge of the mattress when Earl came out of the master bath. "Shit, it's big. God, I want it deep inside me," he murmured as Earl advanced, naked, toward him, the young man's words making Earl's erection harden even more.

The young man lifted and spread his legs. He also spread his arms in total welcome for the mature man's body moving between his thighs. Andy had the condom ready and reached down and used both hands to roll it on Earl's cock, as Earl grasped Andy's ankles and wishboned his legs. Andy rolled up his hips and, still grasping the long, thick shaft in both hands, pulled Earl into him—deep inside him. Andy's hips began to move and so did Earl's. Until now it had been all Andy's instigation, leaving no uncertainty what he wanted from Earl, that he was willing to yield all to Earl.

Earl began a long, deep pump, his mind moving back thirty years to his time with Sandy. Tomorrow he would think about where he was and where he should be going from here. For now he was content to live his past with Sandy.

"Oh shit, oh fuck, I'm gonna come," Andy cried out as he did just that.

So did Earl.

\* \* \* \*

Earl continued for another week, but he couldn't get his deceit out of his mind. Andy's only expressed concern about living with him was an unselfish one for others they might hurt. Earl tried to rationalize that neither his wife nor his children cared where he was and what he was doing— he was unaware of any effort to find him. But he knew that wasn't fair. The women in his family were just spoiled—and he had spoiled them. And he'd done everything he could to keep them from finding him. The secret bank account in itself was proof of his deceitfulness.

His untruthfulness with Andy festered. There wasn't anything in what Andy was doing—he was as yielding and vocally grateful for their relationship as ever. And there was never a hint that he didn't want Earl when Earl wanted him.

After a few days, Earl was increasingly aware that he was letting not just his family but also his workers down by not fighting for his company. As far as he knew Delmarva Pharmaceuticals only wanted his company to gut it and do away with the competition—and its workers. He found he was giving himself the same pep talk of his responsibilities and that he was the one to save the day that his father had given him more than thirty years ago when he hinted that perhaps he would stay in Charleston and not come home to Wilmington to work in the family business.

He had left Sandy then. Toward the end of the week, Earl realized he would leave Andy too—just like he left Sandy. Not because he wanted to but because of his sense of obligation. The inevitability of it festered for a couple of days and then he was gone.

Andy was going to the college in the afternoons now for piano lessons and to practice on his oboe. He seemed quite happy, and the two of them were settling into a routine. They still had sex, but not as often as at first and certainly not with any atmosphere of frenzy, as if it were fleeting.

On the last afternoon Earl took his suitcase to the Lexus and drove out of town, without a look back. He wanted to think he wasn't leaving Andy just as he had left Sandy—without an explanation that he didn't have the fortitude to give face to face. It wasn't like that, he rationalized, because there were five months left on the lease and he had arranged for Andy to be able to stay on in the house, and because he had left a hefty sum of money—enough to see Andy through to the next summer—on the mantel in the living room, with a note assuring one and all that it was Andy's to use as he saw fit.

But, really, it was just like how he had left Sandy. He had been given a second chance at the lifestyle that made him feel alive. And he had given it up.

He made it nearly as far as Georgetown, south of Myrtle Beach, on highway 17 when it hit him how stupid he was. He turned the car around and sped back toward Charleston. He turned the corner of Radcliffe Street, ready to enter the alley behind his row of Simonton Mews townhouses, when he saw Andy get into the back of a limousine parked on the side of Radcliffe. It was Clifford Evans' limousine.

When he entered the house, Earl found his note to Andy crumpled and laying on the floor in front of the fireplace and the money he had left intact on the mantel. Nothing had been taken from the house other than what Andy had brought there with him—including none of the gifts Earl had given him over the past week and a half.

Earl remained in the house for two nights thereafter before getting in his car and driving north. But Andy didn't return. Neither could Earl find him at Club Pantheon in the evenings.

\* \* \* \*

"No, I certainly won't sign it," Earl yelled. He was standing behind his desk at his Washington Street company administrative offices in Wilmington, Delaware, and facing down his bank of lawyers who were telling him that the takeover had been finalized in his absence.

"You weren't here, Earl," his chief lawyer said. "They had all of the cards. Your wife said to go ahead."

"I'm here now."

"It's too late, Earl. Perhaps if you'd been here last week—"

"They will have to take it without my signature," Earl declared.

"Gentlemen. If you give Mr. Hastings and me the room for a few minutes, I think this can be resolved."

All turned to the door, where a member of the Delmarva Pharmaceuticals team Earl's lawyers had been negotiating unsuccessfully with over the past week stood in the doorway to Earl's office.

The lawyers looked displeased and apprehensive. For his part, Earl looked apoplectic. The man standing in his doorway was Clifford Evans.

"It's all over, Earl," Clifford said after the lawyers filed out. "You might as well sign. The opposition is fruitless and, if you don't put an accepting face on it, your employees will start deserting before we can merge the work. If they do, there won't be compensation packages for them."

"You set this up. You and Andy."

"Not Andy. He didn't know anything of what was happening. But, yes, I set it up. Did you think I was giving you a free ride down in Charleston? Surely you knew there would be a piper to pay."

"You devil."

"No, just a good businessman, Earl. Now, I think it would be in your interest to sign the documents. You wouldn't want your family and colleagues to know what you were doing down in Charleston, would you? Do you really want to face that on top of everything else?"

"How did you find me?"

"We do very good research on the companies we acquire, Earl. Our psychologists told us you would likely retreat to where you had been happy in a gay lifestyle. And that's where we found you. Charleston. The research also revealed what sort of man attracted you—and what man you specifically lived with. Both Tony and Andy were selected on that basis. But I repeat that neither of them knew why we were buying their time to service you. And we made it very worth their while to do so."

"You bastard!"

"Just sign the documents, Earl. I'm sorry it had to be done this way. I like you. After you've signed, go home. I think you'll want to go home."

After he signed, Earl didn't feel like staying around in the office any longer—this despite the arrangement being that he would stay on as vice president of the division of Delmarva Pharmaceuticals that his company was becoming. Evans told him he would be needed for the transition, and Earl knew that that was the truth—that it would be very difficult for Delmarva to figure out his company's processes and functions without him. But he had news for them. He'd fight for his employees' compensation packages and all of his energies would go into finding work for any of them who Delmarva wouldn't take. But he wouldn't stay in Wilmington. He didn't know where he'd go, but he could fight for his employees from anywhere in the States.

He got in his car and drove home to the house in Wawaset. His wife wouldn't be there. She obviously hated the house so much that she had already gone to one of her family's homes. And the girls were on summer holiday skiing in Switzerland. His absence had not exactly broken the family out of their normal routines.

As he drove down his street, ready to turn into his driveway, he abruptly stopped and then slowly pulled the Lexus over to the curb. He got out and turned to look toward the sidewalk over the hood of the car, not quite believing what he saw or coming closer for fear that the specter of Andy would vanish before his eyes.

"Hi," Andy said in a low voice.

"God, I'm so sorry, Andy. I never meant to . . ."

"I know. Mr. Evans has told me that my job had been to keep you from going back to Delaware before some sort of business deal went through. I swear I didn't have anything to do with that."

"I know you didn't, but how did you find me?"

"Back in Charleston. When I came to care—not just for the fucking, but to care for you—I found your wallet and looked in it and saw who you really were, where you came from, what your address here was, and . . ."

"And that I lied to you. I deceived you. You found that I had a family. Photographs in my wallet."

"Yes," Andy said in a small voice. He was looking at the ground. "I'm sorry. I shouldn't have looked in your wallet. I just wanted it to be . . ."

"But it wasn't, was it, Andy? I told you I was free—because that was what you wanted to hear and because I didn't want to lose you—and I lied. But you stayed then anyway."

"Yes, by then it didn't matter. By then I would do anything you wanted, no matter who else might get hurt. And I lied too—Mr. Evans told me to. My name's Erick, not Andy."

"How did you get here from Charleston?"

"Mr. Evans brought me. He said something about regretting what he had to do and at least giving you an option. He brought me right here and told me to stand here until you came home. If you didn't come, or if I have to go now, he'll take me to the airport. He's parked down the street."

Earl looked down the street, and, sure enough, Clifford's limousine was parked at the curb.

"And you did that? Even though I deceived you and abandoned you?"

"Yes. None of that matters—at least not to me."

Earl came around the hood of the car and embraced Erick, who no longer was Andy, not caring whether his neighbors saw him embrace another man or not. When they pulled away from a kiss, he put his mouth beside Erick's ear and said, "Can I give you a lift back to Charleston? I have a six-month lease on the townhouse but an option to buy."

"Yes, please," Erick answered. Both men were crying.

Earl heard the engine start up in Clifford's limousine, and his heart raced as the car pulled away from the curb, happily closing out on his options.

# DECOY

"That must be his plane now. Now, remember what you've been told about what your role is." Floris Bourek leaned back in the cushy backseat of the Lincoln MKT Town Car and turned to look directly at the Lebanese beauty sitting beside him. Jamila Maloof, model thin, with long, silky auburn hair, and light-brown, flawless skin, flashed her fluorescent-blue nails in front of her face and effected an expression conveying both boredom and slight irritation. She was dressed in a scoop-necked beige shell and brown jacket over tight stressed blue jeans and fire-engine-red spike heels. She pretty much screamed of being in the profession Floris had hired her to be in.

"Yes, you've told me," she answered back, a bit pouty.

"You've been paid to do it all—either with the man coming in on that corporate jet from Miami or with me—but you are only a decoy so that we can be in public all of the time and it looks like just the two of you are having a good time. But you may not be asked to do anything but have a good time. And when you are told that you need to go powder your nose, you go, and you spend some time at it."

"Yes, I understand."

"Then get rid of the pout. This isn't going to be about paying attention to you."

But it *was* about people paying attention to her and they both knew it. As a decoy she was also to be a distraction. And to any red-blooded man, there was little doubt she'd be a distraction from anything else going on around her.

Bourek turned his eyes again toward the corporate jet that had come to a standstill by a hangar in the private aviation section of Reagan International Airport, the not-so-international-scale airport in Virginia directly across the Potomac River from Washington, D.C. The airport had originally been built in 1941 as a transportation hub for U.S. congressmen and senators who had to travel back and forth between the capital and their voting districts frequently. It was being used now in Bourek's business more for privacy and misdirection. The man they were waiting for had come from London, where he was based, but had flown to Miami to enter the States and on to here, rather than the larger and more alert Dulles International Airport, in the Virginia suburbs, or the Baltimore-Washington International Airport, in the Maryland suburbs.

And there he was, standing at the top of the stairs, framed in the opening into the jet's cabin. Ashur Khoury, the London-based international businessman of Syrian descent. The man who would be flying out again late tomorrow after business talks with Floris Bourek, talks that had to be concluded successfully no matter what it took.

Bourek checked the photograph in the file he held in his hand to make sure the man really was who he was expecting. In this business you always had to check and recheck. Then he climbed out of the car, leaving the backseat door open, and walked over to the bottom of the stairs up to the plane. Ashur Khoury, having checked the photograph in his own file to ensure that the man meeting the plane was the one who was supposed to be meeting the plane, came down the stairs, a smile on his face and his hand extended.

The two spoke briefly on the tarmac, each also scanning the environment to evidence of surveillance, and then Ashur Khoury climbed into the back of the town car, his eyebrows raising and his smile widening when he saw Jamila sitting there.

As the Lincoln drove off, Bourek entered the small private charters terminal. His own car was parked at the other side of that building.

\* \* \* \*

"I thought the capital was a large city," Khoury murmured as the Lincoln glided along. "Yet, we are in the country so quickly." He wasn't really saying this to Jamila. He hadn't said anything to her at all, yet. He certainly hadn't made any move to come closer to her. He'd said it in Arabic and to himself.

So he was surprised when she laughed and answered, in English. "This is called Rock Creek Park. It's a large park running through Washington. It's over three times larger than Central Park in New York City. Do you know that park?"

"Yes, of course," he answered in English, perhaps a little huffily. "You speak Arabic."

"But of course," she answered.

Khoury frowned. He wondered if it had been wise to use a decoy who could understand them if they spoke in Arabic. But then it occurred to him that Bourek perhaps couldn't speak Arabic. Still he was a bit unsettled that this woman could.

Jamila took the hint that she was showing herself to be smarter than many Arab men wanted their women to be.

She went silent and turned her head toward the window and watched the water tumbling through the creek bed running parallel to the road.

But Khoury too felt that this wasn't going as he wanted. He would be with this woman until he got back on the plane. "I thought we were going to go watch tennis," he said in English, trying to use a controversial voice without an edge to it.

"We are. The tennis stadium is on the edge of the park," she answered, turning toward him and giving him a tentative smile. "Do you like to watch tennis?"

"Yes, of course. It was on my list of how I would like to spend the day."

"As I was on your list?"

He didn't answer, and once more Jamila had the impression that she was speaking out of turn. She couldn't help it. She was an American, born and raised in Chicago. It was her parents who had come from Lebanon. And the man's accent told her he was Syrian. Even in the Middle East, a Lebanese woman would not be as diffident with her man as a Syrian woman would be. Bourek had told her just to keep her mouth shut and to play her part. She would do her best to do that, although there were things she naturally wanted to know. She certainly was being paid enough for two days of work to play the role Bourek was assigning her. She lowered her eyes and did what she could to look demure and subservient for the remainder of the drive.

"The stadium looks larger than I thought it would be," Khoury said at length, which was Jamila's signal to look up.

She knew nothing about tennis matches—certainly nothing about professional tournaments—and she realized as soon as the driver opened the door to let her out that she was dressed completely wrong—at least for attending a tennis tournament. Everyone else was dressed for the heat.

48

Her flashy spike heels alone put her out of place. But then she saw the heads of all the men passing by snap around when they first saw her, and she realized that she, in fact, was dressed just right for attention.

Bourek had told her to dress for attention. She didn't ask him why, but she was pleased that, unwittingly, she had succeeded. She put on her oversized sunglasses while the driver handed Khoury their tickets for both the afternoon and evening sessions. They would be arriving near the end of the afternoon session rather than the beginning, but the price, even though high, was incidental to what was at stake in Khoury's visit and his sense of well-being.

Keep the attention on you, not on the visitor, Jamila remembered Bourek telling her, so she stood up straight, pushed her chest out, smiled broadly, and positioned herself a bit in front of Khoury as she walked beside him, his hand possessively gripping her elbow, into the stadium.

Their seats were in a box near one of the corners of the stadium, high up in the box section. There was a group of four chairs, two in front of two. Khoury went into the bottom row first, and Jamila slipped in beside him in the aisle seat. They had entered after the fifth game of an on-serve men's semifinal match. Jamila remained standing as long as possible before play started so that anyone looking over at them would more likely be looking at her rather than at Khoury.

Khoury was voicing his pleasure that the players were both ones he had seen play before when Floris Bourek slipped into one of the box seats in the row behind them.

There was no interaction between the two men during the next two games of play, but at the next sit-down and commercial break, the match being televised live, the two men stood and stretched. A third man, perhaps in his late twenties and gym-trained muscular, stopped and hailed

Bourek as he came up the aisle to the top of the box section.

The two greeted each other as if they were friends, during which Bourek touched the sitting Jamila surreptitiously on the shoulder and murmured that she needed to visit the ladies room. He made a great to do about the young man who had just appeared sitting in the empty seat beside him, but when the young man agreed to, Bourek followed Jamila out, leaving Khoury conversing with the young man over his shoulder.

After two more games, having reached another commercial break, Bourek returned. Khoury and the young man no longer were talking, and when Bourek looked into Khoury's eyes he received a slight shake of the head and shrugged. Jamila returned just before play resumed, leaving three men who had been following her closely to scramble to be seated somewhere before the first serve of the next game. Before the first serve, the muscular young man who had been invited to sit beside Bourek had disappeared.

During the games, Khoury obviously wanted to talk to someone about play. But for some reason he didn't interact with Bourek at all. He was stuck with whispering this and that to Jamila, who did her best to respond in some acceptable way, but, truth be told, she didn't have the foggiest notion how tennis was played and was fighting boredom as much as she could. What she wanted was for the man to show some affection or interest in her or, better yet, tell her more about his business, but he seemed cold in that way. She wondered if Syrian men were all this distant with their women in public. He was a big, muscular man, and she assumed he would be forceful and possessive when they were alone later that night. But why couldn't he show some interest in her now? He made her feel like she was just an object. The fact that she'd been paid to be that—just an object—didn't assuage her slight irritation.

Besides, it was hot out here in the clothes she was wearing. She leaned forward and slipped her jacket off, leaving just the scoop-necked, sleeveless shell. She smiled in spite of herself. Men all around in the boxes were looking at her rather than the play on the tennis court. At least other men here weren't cold toward her.

The match went three sets and ran to where there was only a half hour before the first evening match was to start. Before the last game of the match, Bourek had gone out of the stadium. When he returned he had an order of Pad Thai in a Styrofoam box and a can of beer in his hands, which he left on his chair and whispered, without looking at her, that it was for Jamila—that he and Khoury had business to discuss. To Khoury, he whispered "At the end of the lane on the far side of the Grand Stand court, which is off to our left," and then he left. After a few minutes Khoury was gone too. With a sigh, Jamila reached back and took her meal. She'd be here alone until the next match started. But she'd never really be alone here. There were a hundred eyes watching her. But, by design, they watched her so attentively that they didn't seem to have noticed any interaction between Bourek and Khoury at all.

That was her major purpose here. To be a distraction and a decoy.

They didn't stay long during the evening session. At the break between the first and second set of the first match, a men's doubles semifinal, yet another young man came up the aisle from below, was greeted as a friend by Bourek, and invited to sit with him. And, as before, Jamila discovered she needed to powder her nose and Bourek departed behind her. The feature of starting a new set was that the stadium was closed to returning seat holders for three games rather than two, so Bourek and Jamila were gone for nearly twenty minutes.

The man who had appeared this time was younger than the first, and thinner, and his features were more feminine than masculine. He moved like a dancer. He also was a chocolate brown. He and Khoury exchanged words between the rows up until the break was over, and just before the match resumed, the young black man, named Jared, slipped down into the seat that Jamila had vacated.

When Bourek and Jamila returned, Jamila was left sitting on the upper row of the box with Bourek. The four of them left the stadium for good on the next changeover two games later.

\* \* \* \*

Twilight was marching along although it was barely 8:00 p.m. when the foursome was broken up into three separate, supposedly unrelated segments—the couple of Ashur Khoury and Jamila Maloof and then Floris Bourek and Jared separately—who left the tennis stadium by three separate routes. Bourek had called ahead, and the Lincoln Town Car was waiting in the shadows outside the outer gate to whisk them off. Bourek took the front passenger seat and Khoury sat in the center of the backseat, between Jamila and Jared. There was a bit of touching and whispering in the backseat as they moved north into downtown Bethesda, but everyone was still a bit stiff.

They were taken to the Bethesda Blues and Jazz Supper Club for a late meal and an early start on boozing. There was little talk at the tables as they ate. Only Jared seemed to be mesmerized by the sweet jazz sounds that accompanied the meal, and he did most of the talking, even though they had separate tables. Khoury and Jamila were sitting at one and then, at the table next to theirs, Bourek and Jared. Khoury and Jared were sitting beside each other even though at separate tables, and Bourek had to intercede from time to time when it became too obvious that Khoury was following what Jared had to say and not paying attention to Jamila. Still, Jamila and Khoury sat very close together, establishing to anyone around and not paying deep attention to them that they were a couple.

Bourek and the driver had left the others in the car and checked the supper club out before they'd entered. He had told them that, if something looked "amiss" in the club, only Jamila and Khoury would go in. But they hadn't found anything or anyone in the club to disturb their comfort level.

After a couple of cocktails each and two bottles of wine, they drove back toward downtown Washington to Night Club 9:30, where they loosened up considerably in a crowded room with a hard rock band and free-flowing booze. Bourek wasn't that worried about who might see or listen in on them in this club, because it was hard to tell in a smoky room with high-decibel sound going and strobe lights bouncing off the walls that anyone was with anyone else.

Khoury obviously wanted to dance, as Bourek observed him from the adjacent table, moving his body and feet with the beat of the music. Bourek rose and went behind the table and barked something in the ear of Jamila, who had been just a step or two above passive all night. She shrugged, pulled Khoury up on his feet, and pulled him out to join the morass of people swaying against each other on the dance floor.

After observing the dancing for several minutes, Bourek turned and said something in Jared's ear. Jared smiled and left the table for the dance floor. He too had been dancing in his chair, straining at the bit to be out on the dance floor. After a few minutes, Jamila came back to the adjacent table and sat and found, without too much trouble, where she had placed her vacant stare.

Bourek knew that Khoury and Jared would be dancing close together—and probably touching each other. He wasn't shocked. This was part of the plan. Jamila hadn't been a decoy just in terms of being flashy looking and being a distraction from Khoury and Bourek. It had been made clear to Bourek that Khoury wanted the company of a young man while he was in Washington. But to have gone straight to that in a date for the man for his two days here would have been to invite attention. Attention was the last thing Bourek wanted to invite during his talks to sell surplus arms to Syria through a London cut-out company. Everything about that transaction was illegal, but Khoury's company had demanded to settle the deal face to face.

Beyond knowing that Khoury wanted a young man, Bourek had had no idea what kind of young man. He had provided for two kinds. Khoury had rejected the athletic blond, but he seemed quite pleased with the willowy and somewhat effeminate young black musician.

He didn't care if Khoury and Jared were lost in the tangle of the dancers on the Night Club 9:30 dance floor and were feeling each other out. He knew, though, that Khoury would not come back to the table satisfied with the night continuing just as it was. He left the club room and went back to a more quiet hallway, where he made a phone call.

Where Bourek had stopped to make his call was right outside the door to the men's room. What he didn't know was that in a men's room stall and backing onto the wall just on the other side of him, Khoury had Jared pinned to the wall, the young man's trousers and briefs on the floor of the stall, his legs hooked on Khoury's hips, and his mouth open wide and sucking in air, as Khoury thrust up inside him hard with his cock, again and again and again.

Khoury and Jared came back—hand in hand until they hit the edge of the dance crowd—to their tables and reached immediately for their liquor glasses. Khoury looked happier than he'd looked all day and showed every indication that he wanted to go right back out on the dance floor—and wanted Jared to go with him.

Bourek laid a hand on Khoury's arm, though, and leaned into his ear. "We are leaving—going to the next place."

"But we just got here. I'm having fun here," Khoury said, showing a pouting and obdurate expression.

"You'll like it better at the Green Lantern," Bourek said. "It's a gay nightclub. I've already booked a private room there for you and Jared. They have some interesting toys. After that we'll go directly to the hotel. You can have Jared for the night there."

Beaming, Khoury reached for his jacket that was draped on the back of a chair.

* * * *

Jared was lying in a black-leather sling suspended by gleaming silver chains from the ceiling of a small room with black walls, ceiling, and floor. His arms were stretched up, gripping the chains at the top corners of the sling, and his feet were in stirrups high on the chins at the bottom corners of the sling. His buttocks were raised off the surface of the sling by his own strength as he met and counterpunched the thrusts of Ashur Khoury's cock inside his ass channel. His eyes were big as saucers and his mouth was open and slack from the effort to belt out the yips and moans brought forth by the pounding his was taking.

Khoury, tall and beefy and a bit plump, was standing on the floor between Jared's raised and spread legs. His naked torso was crouched over Jared's and his fists locked on Jared's wrists. He was staring down into Jared's face, savoring the changing expressions  from every thrust, withdrawal, and thrust of the not long, but slug-plump cock.

Both the young black man being balled and the Syrian arms buyer balling him were having a ball.

In the main club room, Bourek and Jamila sat at the same table, sipping their drinks, watching male strippers dancing on poles on the stage, and biding their time. It was obvious that Jamila was becoming increasingly discomforted. She had an exotic look about her that was being mistaken as that of a beautiful transvestite in this gay club, and interested men were floating around, coming ever closer to asking if she was here alone or really was with that bruiser of a sour-faced man who was sitting at a table with her but not interacting with her.

"They've been in there more than a half hour," she hissed. "The Arab is getting what he wants now. Can I go? I can find my own ride."

"Any number of men here would like to give you a lift, Jamila," Bourek said. And then he laughed. "Although they no doubt would be very disappointed to find that you aren't equipped as they wish. And, no, you may not go yet. You have been paid for two days. From your perspective, it doesn't matter whether it's Khoury or me."

"You? You aren't the same as the Arab?"

"Not in any way. It's been very difficult for me to keep my hands, let alone my eyes, off you. When we go back to the hotel, Khoury will no doubt fuck the black guy again—but you, you, Jamila, you'll be all mine."

"I don't think so."

The way Jamila had said that made Bourek look up. The first thing he saw, over her shoulder, were two hulking men in black suits approaching the table. And then he saw the sparkle of light, reflecting off the metal badge Jamila was holding up for him to see, and he moaned.

"You're a Fed?" he asked incredulously.

"Yes, FBI. I wasn't just *your* decoy," Jamila said, a note of satisfaction in her voice. "Floris Bourek, I'm arresting you on a charge of attempted illegal arms dealing."

Two burly men were hauling Bourek out of his chair. "The Syrian. Are you going to—?" Bourek blurted out.

"We'll just leave him to have his fun," Jamila said. "Unfortunately, it's not against our laws for a foreigner to buy arms, just for someone to sell them on American soil."

In the other room, oblivious to having lost their ride to the hotel, Khoury and Jared fucked on.

# DELIVERY

"Sorry about that. I didn't realize it had been on. I'll turn it off."

I reached into my tux jacket pocket and dragged out my cell phone. The Belgian diplomat sitting across the cocktail table from me in the Bourbon Steak Lounge bar of the Four Seasons Georgetown Hotel lifted his hands in a "no problem" shrug and gave me a pleasant smile. We had stopped here for a drink after taking in a concert by the Royal Band of the Belgian Guides regiment at the nearby Kennedy Center. It was Christmas Eve and the whole city was at least pretending to be festive. So was I. It had been my idea to come into the bar when I'd brought him back to his hotel, beckoning him to follow me into the gaily decorated bar, its pulsing red and blue strings of lights bathing the lounge area in the spirit of the holidays.

When I looked at the caller ID, though, I had to change my mind. "Sorry again," I said apologetically, "but this is from a few rungs above me in the pecking order. Since it won't switch over to my inbox now, I'd better take it."

"No problem." Again that hooded-eyes smile that had a touch of something more than just friendliness to it. A slight licking of his lips as he gazed at me. If I'd thought getting tickets on short notice to the concert featuring a group from his own country would be the highlight of his evening, I obviously was wrong. He liked the concert, but he wanted me. I was not unaware that he had his foot out of his shoe with his sock-clad toes rubbing my ankle under the hem of my trousers leg. The rubbing took on the rhythm of the pulsing Christmas lights, which added to the sexual overtones of the act.

It always gave me a little thrill to know I could still have this effect on men.

"Hello, Tyler," I spoke into the phone. I kept my voice neutral. He should know I was working.

"Where are you now, Craig? Are you busy? Jenna wanted me to check on whether you'd brought back her parcel."

"Yes, Tyler, I have it," I answered. "Not with me, though, and I'm not free at the moment, I'm afraid. I can get it to her—" I was taken aback that Tyler would even know about the parcel. For some reason I'd thought Jenna was keeping it a secret from him—like, perhaps, it was a Christmas gift for him.

"Oh, I forgot. Working? Is it the Belgian?"

"Yes, it is," I answered. "I have it and I can—"

"How about eleven tomorrow night then? I should have remembered the Belgian. But now that I see your schedule, I see you should be off for a week after this. Eleven, shall we say? You know where the flat is, don't you? Off Dupont Circle—Q Street."

"Yes, I remember." I hesitated at the word "flat," but it was so like Tyler to use that word rather than "apartment." I'd never been invited to Tyler and Jenna's residence here in D.C. before. I wasn't on their A list by any means. But I had tracked down the street address just because I was curious where they lived. I'd meant to check

60

the place out on Zillow, but I hadn't gotten around to that yet.

Tyler sounded a bit tipsy on the phone. I'd never known him to be the slightest out of control before. The summons I recognized, though—it was quite a slip on his part for him not to have remembered that I was on the hook to entertain the Belgian diplomat tonight—even though it was Christmas Eve. But it was very much like him to have everyone's schedule within reach. And it also was very much like him to expect everyone to drop whatever they were doing to do his bidding.

It was sort of a love-hate relationship between Tyler and me, with me being kept off guard because I never was able to gauge just how he felt about me. And it was important that I know. In many ways Tyler had been my mentor and had helped at strategic junctions to keep me moving ahead in the organization—which was especially hard, considering what my superiors knew about my preferences, not to mention that I often liked to tread my own path rather than the company road. And then there was the inexplicable physical attraction—at least on my part. Inexplicable, because Tyler was really everything fake, but successfully so, that I resented.

There had been hints about Tyler's own preferences around the organization, but they had mostly been stilled when he'd unexpectedly married Jenna, twenty years his junior and no older than or more senior at the time to me in the office. Of course, Jenna had risen faster than I had since that time. I didn't resent that. We'd trained side by side; I knew she was better and smarter than I was—and was far more able than I was to remain on the company road while bending it in her chosen direction. She would have risen that quickly anyway. Marriage to Tyler, though, had made it a sure thing.

I wondered why Tyler, instead of Jenna, was calling me about delivery of what I brought back from St. Petersburg for her. The two usually kept their business separate, and Jenna had been quite careful not to pull Tyler's rank on anything or to try to use him as her go-between. I don't think that would have worked even if she had tried, though. I'd even half thought that what I'd picked up for her in Russia was meant as a surprise for Tyler.

Tyler rarely praised me or my work to my face or within my hearing. I had worked as his deputy in Bangkok, where he'd sent me off to Phattaya Beach for a long weekend with a Russian industrialist the office wanted information from. From that assignment, given and taken without question, I realized that he not only knew my proclivities, but also was willing to use them for office needs. And back here in Washington he was two steps above me, but in the same analysis office.

I had made enemies in the organization—among others as ambitious and opinionated as I was and in the management rung above me—and yet I had gotten a cushy analysis management position for my stint back in the States. I knew Tyler had done that. God knows there were peers of mine who made sure I knew Tyler had done that for me. But he hadn't yet told me to my face that my work was superior—or even adequate to his expectations, which was the same thing as being superior.

Tyler was largely a cipher to me. But I was somewhat afraid that the imperial distance he kept from me stemmed from him not being enough of a cipher to me. In Bangkok I worked with someone who downright despised Tyler and his imperial ways and gleeful filled me in on Tyler's murky past.

"Imperial" is, I think, a perfect way to describe the face Tyler showed to the world. He had a graduate degree from Harvard and had gone on to Oxford and made sure we all knew that—even though, in our business, most everyone else also had graduate degrees from a prestigious university or two. My educational degrees were better than his, for instance, but no one in the office would have guessed it—or would acknowledge it even if the comparison was dangled under their noses.

He feigned a slight English accent to go with the degrees and dressed elegantly as an English don could be imagined to do. He had the tall, thin, yet well-formed body and classic Roman nose slightly pointed toward the sun and sharp, witty tongue to carry it off. No one in the organization wanted to be the butt of a Tyler joke. The jabs invariably bit right through the recipient's armor, which was all the more galling because Tyler's own public persona was so screamingly fake. In total, he came across as everything an elitist Agency senior officer was in the era of the 1950s. That was sixty years ago, though.

I knew from the coworker who had no love for Tyler whatsoever that Tyler was raised on a rural farm in West Virginia, the backwater state where his undergraduate degree had also been taken, and that there wasn't a genuine patrician bone in his body. He had made it to and through Harvard and Oxford and up the ladder in his career by mental brilliance, sterling gamesmanship, and by being able to pass himself off as being part of the Washington inner circle. His first name wasn't even Tyler. It was Earl. Tyler was his middle name and had been his mother's maiden name.

Unfortunately, Tyler knew I knew that, and I'd made the mistake of referring to it in public some years early. His retort had been glib, swift, and brutal, but we both knew it had wounded him and chipped at his façade.

So, what could have either gone to friendship or hatred remained in a limbo of Mexican standoff. I knew his origins were Hicksville and he knew I was, at best, bisexual and, more honestly, gay. There was respect on my part, because he was pulling his part off admirably, if maddeningly. I just couldn't be sure whether there was respect on his part. There must have been some semblance of that, though, or he wouldn't be mentoring me from behind the curtain as he obviously was—while standing off from me in person.

Unless, of course, he had some plan in his back pocket to use me down the road.

At least Jenna had remained as much the Jenna I trained with as the Jenna who was now married to "the man." We had always been friendly, while still competitive, and I sensed no change in her attitude upon having acquired the edge of being married to one of the titans of the office. She wouldn't give me a hint of what he really thought of me—or whether she even knew. Indeed, she gave the impression that he completely compartmented from her what he thought of her coworkers. I gave her credit for not discussing her peers with him; some of our colleagues who I knew she really didn't like were prospering in the office when a little bit of effort from Tyler could easily have sidelined them.

On the whole, despite what some others whispered, I believed that he got, by far, the best part of the deal in the marriage. He needed others to take care of him; he wouldn't stoop to any work that would soil his hands and cause him to break into a sweat—or even to bother to read the directions on how to assemble anything. My vision was of Jenna quietly taking care of him into his old age with a caring, low-key, steady hand—and doing so no matter what feathers he ruffled, including hers.

This just doubled the question running in the back of my mind of why Tyler and not Jenna had called me about the parcel I had retrieved for her in St. Petersburg—

and why he wanted me to bring it their apartment rather than take it to her at the office. What, in fact, was urgent to have it delivered at Christmas if it wasn't a Christmas gift from Jenna to Tyler.

"I said this is the hotel I'm staying at. I have a room upstairs." The Belgian was talking at my inattention. Bad tradecraft on my part.

"Excuse me? Sorry, I was thinking of the call I just got. That was rude of me. I've turned the cell phone off now. You're much more interesting than the piece of business I was thinking of." I gave him a "interested" smile. My attention needed to zip back to the bar in the Four Seasons hotel. I obviously had been daydreaming when the assignment at hand was to keep the Belgian happy.

The Belgian was leaning into the table. He still was playing with my shin, covered in a silk sock, with his similarly clad foot, but he also had a beefy hand on my knee under the table, squeezing it to the rhythm of the pulsing strings of Christmas lights. He obviously knew I would make myself available to him because I was making no effort to draw away from his advances.

He had been more presentable than I had thought he'd be. The top tier of middle-aged, of course, but I appreciated mature men. In compensation, he was tall, and, although "beefy" answered for him well, he also was muscular and not too heavy around the middle. He was no beauty in the face, but we wouldn't be in the light for very long, I imagined. I had known European men like him before. Most of them were experts with the cock, and, so, I was looking forward to this evening. Most of them were just a bit cruel too. I'm embarrassed to say that I also was looking forward to that.

"Yes, yes. You have a room here. That's very convenient." Of course I knew he had a room at this hotel; we had booked it for him. We knew just about everything there was to know about this Belgian diplomat, including what he knew that could be of use to us.

"Would you like to see my room?" he asked. "I know it's Christmas Eve and I've already taken up much of your holiday time . . ." I could hear the eagerness in his voice. It was always nice to be wanted. And of course I wanted to see his room. This had all been part of the preplanned package.

"Yes, I very much would like to see your room," I answered, giving him what I'd been told was a special gift of mine—a dazzling smile of not-completely-feigned eager acceptance. "I can't think of anything I'd rather be doing on Christmas Eve."

\* \* \* \*

Tyler's apartment wasn't what I expected, at least until I got inside. I expected Tyler and Jenna to live on an upper floor with huge windows in some old high-rise apartment building. There certainly were enough of them around Dupont Circle. Instead, it was an old Georgetown row mansion that had been cut up into apartments. Theirs was commodious, with such amenities of yesteryear as wood paneling, wainscoting, and crown molding.

I also expected their taste to be spare, but expensive and in good taste—I certainly saw Jenna this way. As soon as Tyler opened the door to me and I stepped into the vestibule, though, I knew it was a habitat of "one of us." It was chock-a-block with the same collection of Oriental, European, and Middle East treasures that my house was. Everyone in the business seemed to have decided the exact same acquisitions from these places were treasures they must have—to set themselves apart from everyone else. It just had a more "stuffed"—although artfully stuffed—appearance than mine did. That wasn't because they had collected more than I had. In choosing to live in the Virginia suburbs rather than in the thick of the trendy district of Washington, D.C., I could afford twice the house they could on a third of their combined salary.

What was notable was that there was no trimmed Christmas tree or any other evidence of holiday decoration.

Tyler was a surprise, though. He looked as elegant as ever, the handsome face with graying sideburns on a precisely cut head of dark hair. Tall and lean. He had on neatly pressed dark trousers, but instead of a shirt, he was wearing a red silk robe—perhaps his sense of a Christmas decoration? It was more a smoking jacket affair that came down to the knees and, while exposing a good bit of his bare, tanned chest, was held together with a black silk sash. He looked formal and casual at the same time in an old money way that he'd been bringing off for years.

He had a cigarette in one hand and a martini glass in another. The cigarette paper was turquoise. Even in this Tyler had to set himself a step above and apart from everyone else.

"I brought the parcel," I said, as I shook snowflakes off my topcoat and onto the black and white-block linoleum tile of the foyer. The declaration was largely irrelevant, because there it was, being brought from under my arm to be extended toward him.

"You can lay it there on the table," Tyler said, not even looking at the package. "Come on through. What's your poison?"

I stood there in indecision for a few moments, having assumed that this would be the same as his office— that I would be held, standing, in his outer reception area until a secretary came to relieve me of the memo or paper draft I was bringing to him. I had expected that Jenna would answer the door, I'd pass the package to her, she'd thank me for a favor we traded back and forth, there'd be a bit of a chat on where each of us had been in the world that month, and then I'd be gone. I was looking forward to dispensing with the transaction. I also was looking forward to the week without an evening assignment. I could cruise on my own requirements and preferences. I wouldn't have to have any other motives running except the anticipation of personal pleasure.

But Jenna hadn't greeted me at the door for the passing of the parcel. Rather, Tyler, dressed to slouch eclectically and fashionably, as much as Tyler ever did, had answered the door and invited me into his inner sanctum—or at least their entertainment space, devoted, no doubt, to guests who were far more interesting and had far more cachet than I did.

"Well, come on then," Tyler said, turning at the door that I could see led into a well-appointed living room with leather chairs on either side of a fireplace grate. "Just leave the parcel on the center table."

There was, in fact, a round mahogany-wood table in the center of the vestibule, mounted with one of those four-foot-high flower and fruit arrangements that you only saw in hotel lobbies and the pages of *House Beautiful*.

"Oh, and you can just drape your coat on one of the chairs," he called from the other room.

I did as he instructed—I'd always done as Tyler instructed. I left the parcel on the center table and folded my topcoat and left it on one of the four Chippendale chairs set precisely against the vestibule walls between doorways leading off in all directions.

"Perhaps Jenna should open the parcel to ensure that it's what she ordered," I said as I entered the living room. I was self-conscious about being in jeans and a sports shirt; I hadn't thought to dress formal for a package delivery. But, of course, if I'd been thinking on all cylinders, I would have worn an Armani suit.

"Uh, thanks," I then said as Tyler handed me a gin and tonic. I hadn't told him what I wanted to drink, but of course a gin and tonic would have been what I would have asked for.

"Jenna isn't here," he said, as he motioned me to one of the chairs by the fireplace. There was a fire in the grate, and I could see the snow falling beyond the two windows looking out onto Q Street. It seemed to be falling faster than it had when I'd entered the building. I'd had a hell of a time finding a parking space in this area of town, and I wondered how they—or anyone—could stand living in Georgetown under that sort of pressure. But then, in our line of work, pressure and the luck of the find came as givens.

"Jenna isn't here?" I asked as I sat down. Christmas week and they were spending it half a world apart from each other?

"No, she's in Vienna today. Prague tomorrow, I think."

At least there would be plenty evidence of Christmas were Jenna was.

"She asked me to bring that parcel from St. Petersburg," I said. I was speaking repetitive nonsense. But I always had had the feeling of being slow and tongue-tied in the presence of Tyler. It was that superior-subordinate, love-hate thing. He intimidated me and, at the same time, I had been more than a bit distressed when I heard that he and Jenna were getting married. I guess before that I'd hoped the rumors were true and that he secretly fancied me. I know I had secretly fancied him for some time. It had almost been a relief when he had sent me off to fuck and be fucked by the Russian in Thailand all weekend. I thought that, perhaps, it being in the open what I preferred that . . . well, that he'd make some sort of move himself. But he hadn't. And, of course, he would have had to be the one to make the move.

He was as ambiguous about sex as he was with everything else.

And then the surprise announcement that he and Jenna would marry. The office scuttlebutt gave that union six months max—we were used to musical beds and marriages in our organization. But that had been three years ago. And, by all accounts, their marriage was working out marvelously—even though one or the other of them was out of the country a good bit of the time.

"Fuck the parcel," Tyler said, which snapped my head up to where I was looking closely into his face. Tyler didn't use profanity. There was a look of weariness, almost distress, in his chiseled, patrician features. "I invited you here precisely because Jenna was in Vienna today and Prague tomorrow. I, in fact, just spoke to her on the phone to make sure she was there."

"I don't understand," I said.

"Oh, I think you do, Craig. I think you've understood for some time. Maybe you haven't wanted to intellectualize it. But I think you well understand why I called you to come here when Jenna was an ocean and a continent away. This won't change anything, of course. I have no intention of leaving Jenna."

"This? What's this?" I asked.

He just gave me a sardonic "you dunce" look until I no longer could avoid understanding what he meant.

"But . . . why now?" I asked in a low voice.

"I'm tired of shopping on the street, looking for young men who remind me of you and then disappointing me when they aren't you. It's particularly galling during the holidays." His voice sounded strained—as if that was one of the darkest secrets he possessed. And perhaps it was. I had no illusions how hard it was for Tyler to give up a secret. I knew—and appreciated—how hard this was for him.

For just a second, but not more than that, he let the mask drop away from his face and I saw the raw pain and want in his eyes. But it was just for a second, and then we were back to the guarded, patrician Tyler, Harvard and Oxford graduate and office fair-haired boy, whose wit and sharp tongue were a sure defense.

But this was vintage Tyler too, especially with subordinates. He who baldly stated what he wanted—and got it. He wasn't going to beg me, and I knew better than to expect him to. And I wasn't going to walk out of the apartment until he'd gotten what he wanted.

He let his statement hang in the air, as he took a swig of his martini and a couple of drags on his cigarette. I couldn't continue looking at his face, hoping beyond hope that I'd see that vulnerability and want in him again, because it had flickered there so briefly. He certainly knew how to read me, though. I couldn't hide my vulnerability to and want of him in my eyes. So I looked away—to the windows. It was snowing even more heavily on Q Street now. It would be a bear just to get my car out of the parking space on the narrow street and to drive through the drifts across the Potomac to the Virginia suburbs tonight.

Of course I was rationalizing. Which was silly, because there were no decisions for me to make here. This was Tyler—and Tyler's turf.

Tyler stood up from his chair and carefully, deliberately set his martini glass down on the small table beside his chair and placed the red-ash-tipped cigarette— not yet finished, the only signal in the room of his sense of urgency from a man who carefully finished off everything—in an ashtray.

"I'll be in the bedroom when you are ready to come. The main bath is off hallway to the left. Use the beige towels."

He'd left the light on in the bathroom, which was across the hallway from what obviously was a home office den. There were two more doors on either side off the hallway farther on. Two bedrooms, I surmised. I gave a smile, but it was a nervous little smile, when I saw that he had laid out an anal douche bulb on top of a beige washcloth on the bathroom counter. So, he was going to top me. We hadn't cleared that up. It didn't matter to me. I went both ways—and no doubt he knew that. But it was a testament to the sudden impact this had had on me that I hadn't even thought about it.

I certainly had cleared that up with the Belgian diplomat the previous night before we had gone up to his hotel room. But he had wanted it both ways and, after pleading that I be gentle with him, which I was, hadn't come anywhere close to being gentle with me. He had treated me like a common whore and had repeatedly called me that as he was fucking me. And I couldn't say he was wrong. But he had given us what we wanted. So, there were worse ways of being a whore than the one I practiced, I thought.

Night lights were glowing in both bedrooms at the end of the hall. The bedroom on the right obviously was the master bedroom, but I didn't expect to find Tyler in there. And of course I was correct. Even I would have been too uncomfortable having sex in Jenna's bed to perform. The bedroom on the left had two twin beds in it. Tyler was lying on his back on the bed against the far wall. He was covered with a sheet, but I knew he was naked. His trousers and smoking jacket were neatly folded on the bed closer to the door.

He was looking straight up at the ceiling, his eyes glistening. Were those tears?

I had walked down the hall naked and stood in the doorway to the bedroom, backlit by the dim light in the hall. I wanted him to look at me. He could have had this any time in the last eight years. Now that I was here, and our mutual want was out in the open, I could acknowledge to myself that I had wanted him from the first. I knew I looked good and was well equipped. I wanted him to look at me, and I wanted to hear the intake of breath that assured me that he regretted the years of holding back.

I had thought of Jenna while I sat in the living room, briefly watching the fire blaze in the grate of the fireplace and the snow fall and the Christmas lights on the row house opposite blinking on and off beyond the living room windows, bringing rhythmic pulses of red and blue into the room. The rhythmic pulsing of the colors brought to mind the Belgian's hand on my knee in the hotel bar and then of the rhythm of the fuck, and I could see Tyler in that image, but not Jenna. Quite suddenly I saw Tyler and another man. Me? But if Tyler had been seeking it on the street . . .

No, Jenna could just watch out for Jenna herself. I knew a thing or two about Jenna's sex life too. And not just with men. At this moment, I hoped that she had continued with that—that the attraction the two had to each other wasn't dependent on the sexual. But even that didn't matter. Guilt was of no use. Tyler had given instructions. Tyler always was to be obeyed. I could easily envision Tyler very reasonably voicing to Jenna that he had decided to take me on as a male mistress and her answering, "If you wish," and the two going on with their life together just as it was—without Jenna resenting either him or me. Perhaps that too was just rationalization on my part.

He knew that I was there, posed in the doorframe, but he didn't turn to look at me. He wasn't going to give me even that satisfaction.

"Come here," he said. He voice was hoarse. So, at least there was that much. A slight chink in the armor.

I walked slowly over to the bed, as he sat up on the side of the mattress and brushed the sheeting away. This bedroom was on the same side of the apartment as the living room was and the drapes were drawn back on the window, so the same pulsing of the red and blue Christmas lights invaded this chamber.

His cock was long and, like him, on the thin side. And it was in full erection, running up his flat belly as he sat on the side of the bed. His hairless torso, except for a thin patch at the pecs, was that of a runner—lean but well muscled and that of a much younger man than I knew him to be. I had a stab of irritation. Even in this he led a charmed life of fulfilled falsity. I knew his schedule permitted no time for exercise. All of this had been given to him without any effort required on his part. I had to work ten hours a week to maintain my conditioning. And he was twenty years older than me. The man ate whatever rich food he fancied and drank like a fish. I hated and resented that in him. I was no less aroused by him, however, for all of that undeserved reward.

But then I saw them. I'd been told he had them, but, knowing how office legends went, I only half believed. Two scars on his torso, near his left side, just above and to the left of his navel. Bullet wounds. Proof both that his continued life had been charmed and that it had been all too real. Life could get all too real for people in our profession. Seeing the puckered wounds there heightened my arousal, my sense of adventure and risk.

I reached out for the wounds with the fingers of a hand, seeking something raw and genuine in him. But my fingers had barely brushed the scars when he enveloped me with his arms and drew me into his torso, between his spread legs. He buried his face into my belly. I heard the muffled sob and felt the wet tears on my belly. Wrapped my own arms around his neck, my hands cupped his perfectly cut hair; and I kissed the top of his head. We rocked back and forth in place. I felt the urgency of him against my thighs. He no doubt felt mine running up his sternum.

Just like that, all was forgiven. He could have anything he wanted. The chip in the armor was a chasm. He would have possessed me anyway—by right and the power of his position and personality—but I surrendered all, willingly.

His mouth moved down to cover the bulb of my cock, which he sucked between snuffles until we were both heated up and consumed by throbbing need. His lips slid down the shaft, inhaling me, and began to work faster and faster. The pressure and release of his mouth on my cock was matching the pulsing of the Christmas lights filtering into the bedroom. Moaning, I pulled my knees up onto the bed on either side of his hips, leaned my torso back, with my hands gripping his knees; and, using the leverage of my thighs and knees, fucked his throat to an ejaculation.

He released my cock and kissed me along the lower belly line of my trimmed pubic hair after I had come, while I held position straddling his thighs. He handed me a condom packet, which I opened myself and then reached back and rolled onto his cock, which, after my ejaculation, he had slapped around on my buttocks, rubbed across my hole, and used the bulb to worry my hole open to him. I was the one to reach back and lube his shaft and the opening to my channel, as well.

Typical Tyler, I was doing most of the work. I even fucked myself on his shaft, in synch with the pulsing lights, holding the cock in place with a greased hand as I settled on and slid down it and doing the hard riding as he held my waist in his hands and gave me an enigmatic smile.

Just when his remoteness and arrogance were getting to me, though, the dam burst on his emotions. He reached up and pulled my face down and took my lips brutally with his into a deep kiss. He twisted my body to the side and came with me, his knees sliding under my buttocks. Then, still wildly kissing my lips and my face and down to my nipples, he fucked me furiously, with much passionate noise registering need and pleasure from both of us. I certainly learned now that he could use salty profanity as well as anyone could.

The passion ended with nearly simultaneous fireworks from both of us.

He rose from me then and padded off to the bathroom, while I stretched out on the bed. I have no idea how long the uninhibited, honest part of the fuck had lasted, but, for now, it was enough. He had dropped the pretenses and façade—not for long, but long enough for both of us to know he would.

When he returned from the bathroom, he crawled under the covers of the other bed in the room without uttering a word.

I was disappointed, but it wasn't a disappointment that lasted for long. Twice more in the night, his body came down on mine in the twin bed, and he fucked me fully and passionately, holding me in his tight embrace, kissing me all over my body, muttering how hard and glorious my body was, sliding that long, hard cock in and out of me, coaxing out shared ejaculations. Showing each time that he wanted me, couldn't get enough of me, couldn't—in the dark and just between the two of us—voice enough approval of me and my openness to his need.

He became progressively more open and demonstrative with each fuck, until, at the release of the last coupling of the night, he was holding me close, rocking my body with his, and the faces of both of us were tear stained. He didn't leave me then, and we both went to sleep in a close embrace.

I left the apartment before dawn, although dawn came late in the winter in Washington and the moonlight on the fallen snow beyond the windows lit the Georgetown neighborhood up like it was day. Sometime in the night the pulsing red and blue lights from across the street had been turned off. But that was only in the real world. In my memory they were still going, still in synch with the rhythm of the fuck.

Tyler hadn't been in the bedroom when I woke up. I showered, dressed, and came out into the living room. He was sitting in the same chair as the previous evening, smoking an exotic-colored cigarette again, but this time fisting a coffee mug rather than a martini glass. The only other difference was that he wasn't wearing trousers now, just the smoking jacket, with his now-flaccid cock exposed between the parted edges of robe, and he looked more human. His hair was tousled, his arm and hand movements weren't so studied, and his smile when he looked up at me was less judging, less severe than any I'd seen from him before.

"I'll go now," I said, half expecting to be offered breakfast, or a cup of coffee, or something—fearing that I'd receive criticism or a command to never mention this night of coupling again.

"Yes," he answered. No offer of coffee, but no brutal dismissal either. Would he claim that I had seduced *him*? Would this be all my fault?

"The parcel for Jenna is on the table in the vestibule," I said, turning in the doorway into the foyer. "Perhaps you should open it to make sure it's what she expected." I no longer cared if it was meant as a Christmas gift surprise for him. He'd already gotten his Christmas gift—from me.

"Take it with you," he answered.

"Take it with me?" I nonsensically repeated.

"Yes, and bring it back with you this evening . . . and then bring it back every evening until Jenna is back. I'm not sure when she'll return. I made sure your evening work calendar was cleared for a week. If you bring it back every evening, there will be a good reason why you have come to the apartment."

Typical Tyler. He assumed I would be at his beck and call for the week between Christmas and New Years. Like I didn't have other plans and people to see. But of course he was right; I'd clear my schedule for him.

"Yes, sir," I said, my spirits rising as I pulled on my overcoat, put the parcel under my arm, and prepared to face the snow. He wanted a delivery every night for as long as we could—the Christmas gift that kept on giving.

For some reason I felt like I had been the one delivered. Delivered from all those years of secret want. And I was beginning to see the possibility that Tyler might be delivered from himself—or was beginning to be—as well.

"Happy holidays to me," I muttered under my breath.

# Dessert

It had been a grueling six-hour drive from their last stop on Sheila Worthington's nostalgic sweep around the region in which she had grown up before leaving for New York, a chorus line, and then a succession of well-heeled husbands. All of whom heeled over themselves during the parade of decades between. Some of the relatives of the deceased husbands had credited Sheila with their demise, but from where she sat in the bank vaults, humming, she couldn't hear them.

Dominic maneuvered the Jaguar around the last hairpin turn and turned into the long, upward-incline drive that wound around the peak of the mountain overlooking a large lake and several lakeshore communities and up to the resort hotel. Sheila sighed and said, "Let's go ahead and eat at the hotel restaurant right after checking in. When I get to the room, I want to sleep the sleep of the dead."

"Sounds good to me," Dominic replied, forming a charming smile on his pouting-lipped chiseled face and tossing a black curl out of his eye. And indeed it did sound good to him. He'd felt like he'd been on a tight leash for several days now. Sheila was OK, and she paid him well to drive her on this trip—and for other driving services—but, boy could the old babe talk. She'd yakked incoherently for the last two hundred miles about people he barely knew—and felt little loss at not knowing well—at the tennis club where she'd picked him up, dazzled him with an overstuffed pocketbook, bedded him, and planted him in her pool house.

And the thought of her going to bed intent on going right to sleep rather than other things gave him a little thrill.

When they approached the hostess desk at the restaurant, the host gave them a well-trained gaze and assessed them as money and boy toy hunk. He could see that the woman was nearly spent. She was tall and thin and had been quite a looker twenty years earlier, but now her high-fashion clothes looked a bit rumpled, her heavily applied makeup was beginning to droop—along with her bust line—and not every starched hair on her head was behaving. And the hunk, a steamy Latin who looked every bit the nicely muscled tennis pro he really was, was tight as a stretched rubber band and ready to spring in some direction or other in frustration. He'd also given the host an up-and-down look of speculation that the host had long ago identified as possible sexual interest.

Dominic's eyes met those of the host, while Sheila rattled off somewhat catty—but quite accurate—comments on the over-the-top Western style décor of the restaurant perched high over the lake below, the vistas provided being the establishment's best feature. The host gave Dominic a knowing look that permitted Dominic the slight escape valve of being able to roll his eyes in a "women, what can you do with them?" fashion.

With a thought not only to the preferences of his fellow workers but also, he thought, to the preferences and needs of this Latin stud standing before him, the host picked up two menus and a wine list and said, "Come with me, please, I have just the table for you."

It was a very nice table by the window overlooking the vista—which Dominic latched his attention on while Sheila talked about the impossibly spoiled frou-frou dog her friend, Maurine, had just acquired. "You'd think that anyone with white rugs and white furniture—all white décor—would think twice about getting a high-strung Pomeranian that . . ." Dominic didn't so much see the mountainside tumbling charmingly below him to the edge of the lake as that, looking out of the window, he didn't see Sheila with her mouth flapping as she devoured a hunk of pita bread like a cougar having its last meal. And this, of course, was why he was gazing so intently out of the window.

"Wine, beer, or me?"

"Excuse me?" Dominic said, as he turned. There was his waiter standing beside his chair, talking down just to him and smiling. Sheila was lost in her rambling of all of the cleaning supplies Maurine had tried thus far without success.

For the first time Dominic noticed their waiter, who he now remembered as the young man who showed up after the host had said, "Sandy will be your waiter. He'll take good care of you," before he smiled and wafted off.

Sandy. Yes, Dominic could see where the lad had gotten that name. He was a redhead, although it took Dominic a minute for the "he" to register. The voice had been male, if a bit squeaky, but looking closely at his waiter now, Dominic could see that the rest of it was some sort of question mark. He was small of body and wore black tailored trousers and a tuxedo shirt with a ruffle. And he was standing there, hands on hips and slightly bent at the side that Dominic thought of as a "Bette Davis" stance. All he needed was a long cigarette holder in one hand and he'd slip all the way over into the Tallulah Bankhead pose. His face was made up. It was subtle, but he unmistakably was wearing a hint of red lipstick. His hair wasn't long on top, but it was slicked back in an obviously carefully considered "do," and there where long curls over his ears at each side. He was looking at Dominic with an "I just could eat you up" expression in his eyes.

Dominic looked over to Sheila, but she had moved on to rambling about the mistake her friend Dorothy had made in the choice of a tennis outfit or her latest husband. Dominic couldn't gather which it was, and his noncommittal mutterings of ascent seemed to satisfy her and keep her motor running.

Throughout the service, Dominic could tell that the waiter, Sandy, could hardly keep his hands off him and, indeed, he did brush by awfully closely from time to time.

But it wasn't just the waiter, Sandy. Quite frequently, far more frequently than even a famished camel would require, another waiter came by their table, water pitcher in hand, offering to fill Dominic's full glass, with a broad smile or taking away plates one by one when he could have managed all in one trip. This young man was more substantial and a good bit less swishy than Sandy was. He was a tall, well-built black guy, probably a couple of years older than Sandy—and not more than five years younger than Dominic himself.

He was wearing one earring, and his moves were those of a dancer—not nearly as pronounced and given to a fling of the hips as Sandy's moves were, but in a manner that Dominic knew well—and that he found arousing, having frequented a certain gay club often as relief from the duty his pocketbook required of servicing middle-aged women—and men—at the tennis club.

Dominic could tell just by the way that the young black waiter looked at him, that he was interested as well.

And keyed up as Dominic was—all this time on the road with Sheila and no opportunity to pursue the variety of sex he was addicted to—made Dominic go hard and begin to fantasize what he'd like to do with one of these waiters—or both.

At the end of the meal, both Sandy and the black waiter's assistant were standing there, by the table, while Sheila was taking time out from her monologue of society in the town she'd said she wanted to escape for a while, to mull the dessert menu, finally deciding on the crème brulée.

Sandy turned to Dominic with a smile. "And you, sir? What would strike your fancy? We have a special on strawberry shortcake and also on chocolate cake."

"I'm not sure I can decide," Dominic said, with a winning smile of his own. "They both sound so enticing." Both amused and aroused, Dominic had caught on to the double entendres the waiter named Sandy had been dropping. The black waiter's assistant hadn't said anything during the meal, but Dominic was all the more intrigued by him because of that.

"Oooo, I love your accent," Sandy gushed. "And such a rich, deep, masculine tone. Are you from Mount Olympus?"

"No. I'm Spanish," Dominic answered with a laugh. "We don't have a Mount Olympus. Our people are earthy, not heavenly." He could double entendre too, Dominic mused.

"Oooo, that makes me tingle; it just takes my breath away." Sandy preened, fanning his face with a dessert menu. "Well, if you can't decide, then by all means have both, sir. And after dinner may I recommend our rooftop terrace for an after-dinner delight drink and gazing at the stairs in our clear sky here. It's really quite private."

"I'm much too tired for anything after dinner," Sheila said.

All three men turned and stared at her. There had been no warning that Sheila had cut off her monologue and

83

was now paying any level of attention to what they were saying. She had made her statement with a completely innocent face, though, and hadn't followed up with anything but her own preference for sleep rather than any after-dinner activities, so the two waiters dropped back a step and went invisible, leaving it to Dominic to pick up the conversation with her. In any event, the invitation had been laid on so heavily that Dominic could hardly have missed it.

"Well, we'll just get you settled in the room then, and I'll bring my laptop back to the library they have here and check my e-mails and do some catching up," Dominic answered with a concerned voice. "You get your rest, Sheila. We have another 250 miles to drive tomorrow afternoon."

Less than twenty minutes later, Chocolate Cake knelt between Dominic's thighs on the rooftop terrace and gave Dominic's nicely proportioned cock expert suck, while Dominic held Strawberry Shortcake at his side, a hand on Sandy's buttocks with fingers snaking into his channel and his other hand stroking Sandy's pert little cock.

Sandy was making little high-pitched babbling sounds, which Dominic stopped by taking the little waiter's lips in his, forcing them open with his tongue, and swabbing Sandy's tonsils.

Strawberry Shortcake panted and whimpered as Chocolate Cake reached over and pulled his trousers and briefs off his legs and then held Dominic's cock erect and steady as Dominic lifted Strawberry Shortcake up, turned him around, and swung his leg over Dominic's lap. Together, Dominic and Chocolate Cake settled Strawberry Shortcake on Dominic's cock as Sandy writhed and babbled a range of contradictory short, breathy statements: "slow, slow, slow, hurry, all of you. Oh god, god, oh god. You'll kill me. Yes, yes, yes."

Together, Dominic and Chocolate Cake, with Dominic palming and spreading Strawberry Shortcake's butt cheeks and Chocolate Cake holding Sandy at his waist, lifted and lowered him on the full length of Dominic's cock until he stopped writhing and started to moan and beg for the fuck.

Dominic stood then and walked slowly around the terrace, raising and lowering Strawberry Shortcake on his cock, while the young redhead clung to his midsection and groaned and gasped—and, in short order, fountained his ejaculation.

Then Dominic gently lowered the redhead to the deck of the terrace and turned, strongly erect still, not himself in flow, not yet satisfied, opting now for Chocolate Cake for dessert.

Chocolate Cake stood and turned fully toward Dominic, smiled, leaned his rump back on a terrace table, and started to unbuckle his belt.

Dominic strode deliberately toward Chocolate, giving him time to drop his trousers. And, that done, he moved faster, grabbed Chocolate roughly—as Chocolate laughed a hearty laugh—turned him belly down on the top of the table, used one hand to establish purchase of his cock head inside Chocolate's gaping hole and used the other hand to lock one of Chocolate's arms behind his back.

"Yes, yes, Fuck me hard!" Chocolate cried out in a rich baritone—the first thing Dominic had heard him say all evening—as Dominic slammed his cock up inside Chocolate's wide channel. This was the tension reliever Dominic wanted. This was what would unwind him from all those miles on the winding mountain roads today "yes ma'aming" and "no ma'aming" to Sheila's inane conversation.

And Chocolate Cake, well muscled and sturdy and robust, cried out that he wanted him rough and deep—and with pneumatic force. Dominic leaned his torso down over Chocolate's back, Chocolate threw his free hand back and laced it around Dominic's neck, and they turned their faces to each other in a deep kiss as Dominic pumped, pumped, pumped.

Strawberry Shortcake moved behind Dominic and grabbed and squeezed his butt cheeks and helped maintain the rhythm of the fuck. Chocolate Cake also was helping, essentially fucking himself on Dominic's cock with long backward thrusts of his hips.

All three cried out as Dominic came. He backed up and plopped down in a chair, while Chocolate Cake turned and lifted Strawberry Shortcake up, laid him down on his back on the table top, slapped the little redhead's legs aside, thrust his own hard cock inside the channel Dominic had so recently reamed for him, and started to fuck him with a frenzy that had the little redhead sliding back and forth on the surface of the table. After a short breather, Dominic approached Chocolate from the rear again and Dominic fucked Chocolate Cake while Chocolate fucked Strawberry Shortcake, bringing on a triple ejaculation.

Sheila was already asleep when Dominic came into the hotel room and climbed into bed that night. But half way through the night she was rested enough to nudge Dominic onto his back and fondle his cock and balls enough for him to attain an erection in a half-awake state, and then she mounted him. Exhausted, Dominic let Sheila drive.

The next morning, a now-fully alert Sheila, a sleepy and nearly hobbling Dominic in tow, arrived all cheery smiles and gushing accolades in the hotel dining room for breakfast.

Once again a more-than-eager Sandy was their waiter, backed up by a big-smiling black assistant waiter.

As their breakfast was coming to an end and Sheila was babbling about how she wanted to change the curtains in her living room, Sandy leaned down and said sotto voce to Dominic, "Would you have time after breakfast for some dessert, sir? The roof terrace is a great place for dessert and coffee in the morning." Chocolate Cake was standing behind him, looking ever so hopeful.

Dominic raised his eyes, a response on his lips that no doubt would be a classic, but that has been lost to history.

Sheila suddenly stopped running at the mouth, and in a clear, steady, not unfriendly tone, said. "I wouldn't suggest two this morning, dear heart. If you must, I'd suggest just the chocolate cake. It looks more substantial. I was rather hoping we'd indulge in our own dessert of fine old port and cheddar cheese when we returned to the room—and what I was served last night was a little limp from too many sweets."

# DISILLUSION

Rick could hear the rich tones of Jason Jenkins' speech to his volunteers in the bull pen down the hall over the nearer-to-hand grunts of Herald Hastings. The young college student's belly was pressed into the Xerox machine flap in the copy machine at campaign headquarters, and the candidate's chief of staff was crouched over his rump, hands grasping his hips, and was thrusting hard and in a fast rhythm up his back channel. The trousers and briefs of both of the men were bunched around their ankles. Otherwise they both were fully dressed in the spiffy suits they were wearing to this "rah, rah" session, where Jenkins was rallying his campaign workers to push harder toward an election victory in six weeks.

Jenkins was running for a congressional seat that had become more available because of the long-incumbent opponent's heart attack and death. Another candidate from the congressman's party had been thrown into the breach, but it was late days for him to gain the recognition that Jenkins had now, and the highly photogenic Jenkins had flipped up seven points in the polls.

Hal Hastings covered Rick's mouth with a hand when his thrusts were deep and reaching climax so that no one would hear any loud noises of being taken quickly and hard coming from the Xerox room. He wasn't particularly big—and Rick had little trouble taking him—but he was vigorous. The door was shut and locked, and few had keys. Everyone else should be in the larger room that was called the bull pen. Hal wasn't being missed, as he and Jason had agreed as a matter of strategy that the chief of staff, who was the real power in this campaign, wouldn't be seen hovering over the candidate. And Rick wouldn't be missed because he'd been assigned the privileged position of manning the telephone in Jenkins' office during the assembly. There should be no one needing to make copies of anything during the Jenkins' speech.

To the sound of applause and a few raucous cries from the other room, Hastings released Rick's body, pulled out and away from him, and stepped back. Rick remained where he was, bending over the Xerox machine, and breathing heavily, as Hastings pulled the filled-out condom off his cock, set it down on the flap of the copy machine beside Rick's chest, pulled his briefs and trousers up, zipped up, and secured his belt.

Indicating the spent condom, Hastings said, "Take care of that, please, Rick. And don't leave it anywhere here at campaign headquarters."

He turned and unlocked the door to the reception area for his and Jenkins' offices. He paused for a moment at the door.

"Oh, and I came back here to tell you that Jason wants to meet with you after he's done his glad-hand pass-through of the bull pen and survived the obligatory tasting and snapshots with Sally Ann's oatmeal cookies."

"Me? He wants to talk with me?" Rick asked as he pulled his own briefs and trousers up his legs.

"Just go sit in his office. You were supposed to be manning his telephone anyway."

"Yes, sir," Rick answered. But Hastings was already gone—out to the bull pen to be in the background for those oatmeal cookie shots, looking as if he'd been somewhere in the area all along.

Rick didn't resent the man. Not really, or not too much. He was a cold-blooded snake, certainly, but he had to be to do what he did for political candidates. And he did what he did very well. Rick wasn't so dumb or unobservant not to know that, if Jenkins won—and it now looked quite likely that he would—Herald Hastings had made all of the difference. So anyone who wanted Jenkins to win needed to be nice and accommodating to Herald Hastings. Or so Rick's justifying mantra went.

Hastings had been straight with him on the fringe duties of Rick's job as the coordinator of the college-age volunteers. He had fucked Rick even before he'd offered him the job. Rick hadn't reported it, even when it continued after he'd gotten the position. He saw Jason Jenkins as being so upright and straight laced that he surely would have fired Hastings on the spot and would have done little to try to cover up why. Even Rick could see that this would be the death knell of Jenkins' campaign. Hastings was just too closely identified with this run at Congress. And Jenkins had to win. He was the only completely honest and incorruptible politician Rick had seen in the state—ever.

In addition, Rick needed this position. He was studying political science at the university. This was his sophomore project. He needed this to satisfy his project requirements and for the A grade it guaranteed him. And he was gaining experience and networking he'd need for when he got into politics himself. He wasn't so dumb as not to know there were Herald Hastings types in this business. But he also knew there were damn few Jason Jenkins in this business. Rick couldn't rock that boat.

Besides, Rick was actively gay and a bottom. He'd never done it for a guy as old as Hastings before, but Hastings wasn't a toad. And he had good technique. Rick couldn't say that he wouldn't have gone with Hastings for a bit of money even without everything else Rick was getting out of this experience—including the protection and support of Herald Hastings.

And now Jason Jenkins had asked for a meeting with Rick. He sure hoped that wasn't about what was going on between Hastings and him.

\* \* \* \*

"I wanted to see you, Rick, because the campaign is entering a new phase, and we must do what we can to maintain momentum."

"Yes, sir. Whatever I can do to help." And Rick meant it. He was all aglow to be sitting here alone with Jason Jenkins in the candidate's office. Well, not completely alone. Herald Hastings was sitting off to the side and looking through some files as if he was only half listening to what Jenkins was saying.

Jenkins was mesmerizing. He was a tall, strongly built man, with wavy black hair, twinkling hazel-green eyes, and a smile that never stopped. He had a knack of devoting his full attention to the one he was talking to, and if he was talking to a group of three, each of the three felt like he was focused just on them.

That's the way Rick felt now. The candidate reached out with a strong hand, with long, sensuous fingers and carefully manicured nails, and touched Rick lightly on the forearm. Rick felt a chill go all of the way up his back. This intimate touching wasn't what Jenkins did for Rick alone. He was a touchy-feely sort of guy. He connected with everyone this way. And Rick thought everyone felt the same chill he did. If Jenkins were able to directly connect with every constituent in the voting district, Rick had no doubt the candidate would win by a landslide.

Rick briefly wondered if everyone else Jenkins touched would be willing to lie down on the carpet right here in the candidate's office and open their legs to Jenkins. Rick would—he worshipped the man that much—but he couldn't speak for anyone else. He must not have quite this effect on others, though, Rick thought. There wasn't a hint of sexual scandal floating around on the man. Politics was ripe for such rumors—manufactured and otherwise—but Jenkins was squeaky clean.

Sort of a pity, Rick thought, having gone hard from just the touch on the arm and the warm smile.

"I need you to recruit more college students to canvas for the campaign, Rick," Jenkins said, bringing the young campaign worker out of his reverie. "We need maybe twice what we have now. Young, good-looking men, like yourself. This is a walking-the-street job, so no women. It's not safe on the streets for them, alas. That's something I plan to fix when I'm in office. And all clean-cut and good-looking—like you. We want to impress the voters, not scare them off."

The young campaign worker was flattered and was practically humming from the attention and the faith Jenkins was placing in his hands.

"Sure, I can do that, sir. I'll get right on it." Rick was fairly trembling at the favor the candidate was bestowing on him—and the confidence. He had no idea how he was going to muster up thirty more campaign workers from the university campus. But the fact that Jenkins was ahead in the polls and they were coming close to the election would help him. College students talked like they favored the underdog, but they were more likely to hop on a rolling victory bandwagon like Jenkins' campaign was becoming.

"You have a dinner meeting with the big donor, Mrs. Engles, Jason," Hastings said from across the room. "You'll not want to be late for that."

"Of course," Jenkins responded. "Mustn't keep the money waiting." He stood, with Rick struggling up to his feet as well, flashed a broad, melting smile just for Rick, and held out a hand.

"Oh," Rick muttered, with a gulp, realizing that Jenkins wanted to shake hands. He quickly rubbed his hand dry on his hip, and reached out. The candidate's grip was strong. It sent an electric pulse up Rick's arm.

He was at a loss on who should leave the room first but then decided that it must be him. But as he turned toward the door, Herald Hastings said, "Could you stay back for a few minutes, Rick? There are some particulars of the assignment we should go over."

"Yes, of course," Rick mumbled. He looked around for a last, admiring glance at Jason Jenkins, but the candidate already had left the room. He sank back down into his chair, in awe of the experience he had just had. He'd never been this close to Jenkins before. He had never realized the man could have this effect on him—a sexual one. He ached for him.

"You understand what Jason is asking you to provide, don't you, Rick?"

"Yes. More college-age campaign workers. To do door-to-door canvassing. All men."

"Yes, but more than that, all good-looking. Blonds. As many of them blonds as possible. They make the best impression."

Rick took a little umbrage at that. He was dark. He didn't see why people would be willing to open their doors for a campaign pitch from blonds any more than they would from dark-haired men, like him.

"And the blonds. I want them to be just like you—as cooperative as you are."

"But I'm not a blond. I don't see . . ." But then he did see. Hastings wanted variety. He wanted Rick to recruit blonds who would let him fuck them.

"Do you understand?" Hastings repeated.

"Yes, sir, I do." And he did, or at least thought he did. And he'd somehow manage to find what Hastings wanted. He knew how important Hastings was to this campaign, and Jason Jenkins had to win this election. Rick wasn't going to be any part of him not doing so.

"Good. Now close and lock the door, please, and come over and lean over the desk and drop your trousers."

That night, in his dorm room, already having recruited five campaign workers, including two good-looking and willing blonds, Rick drifted off to sleep, masturbating himself and dreaming of Jason Jenkins pressing his knees between Rick's thighs. Crouching over Rick's body, with his fists buried into the sheets on either side of Rick's waist, the Jason Jenkins of the dream was capturing Rick's eyes with his, smiling that mesmerizing smile. Rick flinched, grunted, and then sighed, as Jenkins entered him and then started slowly to pump. He was thick and long, just as Rick knew he'd be.

Rick woke with a start, having just ejaculated and sent cum spouting on his belly and the sheets on either side of him.

He felt shame at thinking of the squeaky clean candidate that way. But he couldn't help it. The man was just so sexy and arousing. Hastings paled in contrast, but Rick had to accept that what he got out of this was Hastings, not Jenkins. And, of course an A for his political science project.

\* \* \* \*

The day out canvassing a town at the southwest corner of the congressional district had been a long one. But it had been fruitful, with more residents willing to say they were voting for Jenkins than the campaign prognosticators had projected. There would be press interviews the next day, and the projections that would be used would be those of the prognosticators unless Rick could get the statistics he collected today back to the office that night.

There was nothing to do but for him to drive back to campaign headquarters in the wee hours of the morning and slip a manila envelope with the statics under the door, to be found in the morning.

When he got to the office, though, he found that the front door was unlocked and lights were on in the bull pen. He entered and walked through that toward the executive offices. He'd leave the envelope under the door to the reception room for Jenkins' and Hastings' offices.

But that was unlocked and open too, and a few lights were on in the reception room. Still, the light was dim in there. Not so in Jenkins' and Hastings' offices, though. Lights were blazing in there. There must be a cleaning crew in, he thought. He had no idea what nights the offices got cleaned.

He'd leave the envelope on Jason Jenkins' desk.

Bad idea, though. When he got to the door, he found himself pulling back into the shadows of the reception room in shock. All that he had thought—all of his illusions—about Jenkins shattered in one glance.

Jenkins, naked, was sitting in a Chippendale armchair. Straddling his lap, also naked, was a young blond man. Todd, one of Rick's recent recruits. He was sitting in Jenkins' lap, facing him, his legs straddling the arms of the chair. Jenkins was holding his waist on either side and pulling the young blond up and down on his cock.

Todd had been recruited for his willingness—and that had been conveyed to Herald Hastings, with the understanding that Todd would be servicing Hastings.

Not Jenkins. Not squeaky clean Jenkins, the man with a sterling reputation, a perky wife, two darling children, a cocker spaniel, and two Siamese cats.

Yes, Rick had fantasized, but that was all it had been. And this. A shocking disillusion.

Rick gave a jerk as a hand closed of his elbow on either side from behind him and he was being pulled, backward, into Hastings' adjacent office.

"The blonds . . . they were for—" he blurted out, when he saw that it was Hastings pulling at him.

"Jason, yes."

"But I thought . . . I mean, why did I have to procure others for him? I would have loved—"

Disillusion number two. "Jason is partial to blonds. I offered you, but he wasn't interested. I'm the one who likes them with black hair, like you."

# DOUBLERS

I knew where this was going.

I was sitting in Kamrod Tikka's lap, both of us naked, me facing him, and with my heels resting on the headrests of the adjacent seats and my back braced against the back of the seat in front of us in his business jet high over India en route to Bangkok.

He already had his fat cock up inside me, and I felt his hands go under my buttocks from each side and my buttocks spread and a finger from each hand enter me as well. I was grabbing the headrest on both sides of his head for dear life to stay in place as his hands no longer were encircling my waist.

I moaned as a second finger from each hand penetrated me as well.

"You liked the copilot, didn't you?" he murmured to me. "I can have him back here in a minute. I know he'd like it. Two cocks inside you at once; two men giving you close attention. We've done it before."

"No, Kam, not now, please. Maybe someday, but . . . oh god, oh god!"

A third finger from each hand had entered me, and he had grasped his shaft with his fingers and was moving it back and forth inside me.

"I have enough fingers in you in addition to my member now that the copilot would not be any more taxing. You can handle it."

I panted and gasped . . . and came up his hard, dark belly in the rivulet of black, curly hair that descended from his chest into his pubes.

Kamrod wasn't done, though. He was only beginning. He had superb control. The fingers came out of my channel and he was grasping my buttocks and pulling them apart. With the strength of his strong arm muscles he was raising and lowering me on his shaft too, until, finally, as the jet started its descent into Bangkok and I nuzzled my face into the hollow of his neck and gasped and moaned, he gave me his seed in three prodigious jerky bursts.

I lay against him, panting, while he ran his hands up and down my back and went flaccid inside me. I whimpered for him, letting him know he had mastered me. I knew it was what he wanted. India putting America in its place.

I even asked him to do it again in a low whisper of longing, knowing there wasn't time before we landed, but also knowing it excited him to have that control over me and that well into his fifties he could still have a twenty-two-year old blond beg for it from him.

"You are ready for the copilot too?" he asked, his voice thick with lust.

"No, Kam, not yet, please. Just you. Again."

I felt him stiffening again at the thought, but then there was a ding, the red light went on over our bank of chairs, and he muttered with regret that I'd just have to wait—that we were descending into the Thai capital.

"Just so you know, though," he said. "You are ready for two—and two of respectful girth. Whatever happens, I want you to know that and not have fear on that account."

I took his face in my hands, kissed him, and wiggled my butt on his shrinking cock, as if I wouldn't listen to reason. And I knew that this excited him as well. I needed to keep him excited.

I knew he wanted to double me. He'd been building up to it for some time. He talked of it often—even said he was in an international club that practiced it. But I had fended that off. I didn't know how much longer I could do that. If I truly didn't want to give in to it, I'd have to find another daddy. And it would be hard to find another man in Mumbai as hard bodied, hard cocked, and rich as the international entrepreneur, Kamrod Tikka. And not having my passport in my possession, Mumbai was pretty much my selection pool.

He had picked me up in a male bordello in Mumbai after I'd been there less than a week, abandoned by the American businessman who had brought me there and suddenly decided he preferred dark-skinned Indian boys to American beach bum blonds. I had been told that I could work as a male escort, with the wining and dining taking up more time than the fucking.

I had gone with Kamrod willingly, because after a week in the bordello, and discovering that young blond men were in high demand in India, I didn't know if I could survive another week in that place. On the whole, I'd found Indian men small cocked, but they had some peculiar notions of what to do with their cocks. And the Western businessmen who visited the brothel wanted their money's worth and generally wanted rough sex that they didn't think they could get away with in their home environments.

Kamrod had been both the hunkiest and most refined of technique of the Indian men who had bought my time, and he took his time with me. He also took me out on the town before bedding me, giving me more of what I had expected as a male escort.

What he didn't do was keep secret from me that he enjoyed three-way, double penetration sex, and wished to include me in that. I found the fingers plus cock routine he liked painful at first, but I'd been with him a full month now, and one night I'd even managed most of his hand buried and gripping and rotating his cock inside me. He took it slow and gave me plenty of time to adjust.

But each time he'd asked me if I was ready to include another man, and each time so far I'd managed to hold him off.

He was tall and burly for an Indian. A handsome face and an assured manner. He was dark skinned, telling me that he was from south India, where that was normal. And I liked the black, curly body hair he had on his forearms and thighs and cascading down from his Adam's apple to his cock. He was fastidiously clean, smelling always of cinnamon and a heady incense.

His mouth was sweet and persistent on my cock, and he could play me for nearly an hour at a time, bringing me to the brink and then holding me off. Then suddenly entering my channel with three or four fingers and spreading them and making me come in a flood as the pad of a thumb thrumbed on my prostate. Sometimes that was the end, but more often, he'd move between my legs then, and I'd feel his thick cock entering me between the fingers and he'd work me for another eternity, showing that he knew how to control himself as well.

And, as I said, he took his time and made love to me with his voice as he fucked me. He had a mesmerizing tone to his voice and he could speak in the rhythm of the fuck. And each time he told me that it would be much more sensual when there was another man.

I was never quite sure how long he would want me. He seemed the type who could keep in thrall a young man of his own choosing from his own business world and who didn't need to go to a brothel.

I actually saw that in the first week I was with him in his home. A young German man, who obviously, at his initial appearance, didn't like Indians and who visibly pulled away from them and showed distaste at their touching manner, came—reluctantly, I'm sure—to Kamrod's house for a business meeting and no more than two hours later was coming on a toilet stool, his ankles on Kamrod's shoulders, and melting at the love Kamrod was making with his voice in the young man's ear and with his cock in the German's channel.

Soon thereafter, I observed the German sandwiched between Kamrod and another Indian on a low-platform bed, servicing both of their cocks in his channel and obviously having gotten over his aversion to Indians. The other Indian, large boned and large cocked lay on the bed on his back, with the German stretched out above him, and his powerful arms laced under the German's armpits, holding the German's arms trapped up and away from his stretched torso. Kamrod was between the German's legs, with the German's ankles on his shoulder, and Kamrod's cock moving slowly in and out of the German's channel above the fat cock of the other Indian. The German's head was lolled to the side, his mouth was open and slack, his eyes seemed swimming in cum, and he was moaning quietly to himself.

Later, as he was fucking me, Kamrod asked me if what I saw appealed to me, and I tried to be as noncommittal as I could be without angering him or prompting him to send me away. In truth, though, I did find at least the theory of it arousing.

I asked, apprehensively, why he had brought me from the brothel—and then not just discarded me when he'd done all he wanted to do to me. He told me that he had heard about me from a colleague and that I was just the kind who turned him on. He also smiled and said he hadn't done everything he wanted to do with me yet, causing me to shudder as much from the way he'd said it as from the touch of the backs of his fingers gliding up the inside of my thighs.

He more than hinted that he liked threesomes and double penetrations, but I didn't hop on that suggestion. Increasingly, though, I figured I'd either have to show interest in that or find another way home from India.

I was in India illegally now. I had no papers. Whatever man I was with could pretty much do anything he wanted with me. I felt lucky that Kamrod, hunky, not too old—maybe early fifties—refined, and filthy rich was the man who had me.

When he said he had to go to Bangkok on business and he wanted me to go with him, there wasn't much I could—or wanted to—say other than yes. I started to mention the problem of leaving the country, but he produced my passport, which he somehow had managed to acquire.

He didn't give it to me, though, and I didn't ask him to.

We were booked at the Oriental Hotel, Bangkok's most prestigious hotel.

That night, in a tenth-floor suite, Kamrod was all about my needs rather than his. Although he was a good lover, everything we'd done before was because he wanted to do it. On this night, though, he wanted to know what I wanted. He said we could just sleep too, if that was my wish.

I would have liked the "just sleep" suggestion—Kamrod was quite virile and had fucked me at least once a day since he had, essentially, bought me from the bordello.

But knowing his appetites, I didn't want to do anything that lessened his ardor for me.

So, I asked him to take me out onto the balcony overlooking the Chao Phya River, with the Wat Arun temple lit up across the water, and lay back on the chaise lounge out there, while I mounted him and fucked him slowly and gazed out over the exotic river scene, the water still alive with small long-tail boats even in the night.

He seemed pleased with my choice and came twice for me. Still, in the end he reminded me that I was prepared for so much more.

The next day, he was in meetings until the evening. I sat by the pool, where I got several propositions—from men and women alike. But it was nice not to have to say yes. Except for a young, small Thai pool boy, who assured me that he was in his twenties and who I fucked down in a patch of bougainvillea near the river's edge, happy to be the top for once, in a very long while. I politely turned aside all other offers.

Near sunset, Kamrod came back to the room and told me we'd be dressing formally for dinner and that we'd be eating with the Belgian businessman he had come to Bangkok to strike a deal with. I didn't ask what sort of businesses Kamrod was in—and he didn't tell me. I surmised there was more than one business, though, and I could tell they were lucrative.

As we were leaving our suite for the hotel's Le Normandie restaurant, Kamrod leaned in to me and said, "I believe I have the deal I want, but he has expressed an interest in you. I need for you to be pleasant to him— despite whatever impression he makes."

Of course, I thought. Why wouldn't I be pleasant? But then I met the man. Kamrod introduced him as Hugo Jaguerman. I would have thought that Pig would be a more fitting name.

He was a massive man, even bulkier than Kamrod. But I could tell by the way that he filled out his tux shirt that it was mostly muscle, not fat. His jacket must have been specially tailored for him to accommodate the girth of his upper arms. His head, a pig's head, complete with snout, seemed to lay directly on his shoulders. What little I could see of his neck was as thick as his head.

He was bald, with folds of fat at the base of his neck, and his ears looked like those of a pig also. His eyes were small, buried in puffy cheeks, but as he squinted at me, I could see the same expression of lust that I'd seen in men's eyes most of my life.

He ate like a pig too, his eyes rarely leaving mine, as he chewed noisily on all of the artistically prepared dishes that were wasted on him.

He and Kamrod talked—although Jaguerman looked at me rather than Kamrod. But they spoke in French, which I didn't understand. I was disgusted with how the pig would stuff his mouth and then talk. He left the impression of a coarse man with huge appetites that were almost impossible to satiate. I shuddered at the thought of what I assumed I was there for.

Hearing French coming out of such a hoggish face was a surprise. But he was Belgian, so I suppose it was natural that he'd speak French. It was more of a surprise that Kamrod spoke it—and when he spoke it, it sounded like music. A little chill went up my spine at the thought of him speaking soft French in his mesmerizing voice while he fucked me.

When the coffee was served, Kamrod stood up from the table and walked away without a word to me, although he leaned down and spoke softly in Jaguerman's ear, which was answered by a leer.

And Kamrod didn't come back to the table.

"We go now," Jaguerman said in heavily accented English when he'd finished his coffee.

"Mr. Tikka?" I answered in a surprised voice.

"We will meet him at apartment."

I started to object, but a burly man in a black suit was at the side of our table. He had a chauffeur's hat tucked under his arm and seemed to be well known to Jaguerman. I got that he was Jaguerman's driver and that I indeed was going someplace with Jaguerman. The Belgian alone was muscle enough to manage that even if I didn't want to, but here in the best restaurant in Thailand, his bulky chauffeur made clear that I shouldn't make a scene.

I knew for sure now what Kamrod meant by being pleasant to the Belgian businessman. And I probably knew exactly why I'd been brought along for the jet ride. I would not be surprised to find out that the Belgian had specified what type of young man he wanted Kamrod to bring with him from Mumbai and that this was what prompted Kamrod to take me from the brothel.

The thought struck me that I would not be flying back to India with Kamrod. But this was quickly replaced with the fear that I would not be leaving wherever I was going now alive.

In the back of the Mercedes limousine, where I half assumed I would be thoroughly fucked, I wasn't.

I sat in the middle of the backseat, and Jaguerman, taking up much of the width of the seat, sat across from me, stared at me, and picked at his teeth with a toothpick.

"Let me see it," he said in a low growl.

"See it? See what? Oh." He was motioning with his hands what he wanted to see.

I spread my legs and unzipped my trousers and fished my cock out.

I cupped my balls in the palm of my hand, and we sat there for several moments, Jaguerman picking his teeth with a toothpick with one hand, his legs now spread too, and his other hand holding himself through the fabric of his tux trousers.

I assumed this was the start of rough sex. But it wasn't.

"Enough," he said, and I folded my goods back into my trousers and zipped up. He kept his hand on his crotch, though, and it was obvious he was aroused.

We didn't have long to drive after that—to yet another high-rise building on the banks of the Chao Phya.

Jaguerman lived in the penthouse, which, although large, was surrounded on all four sides by terracing that dwarfed the apartment.

I held back a gasp when we entered the apartment and he flipped on the light switch.

The lounge room we entered, with an S-shaped sofa winding its way through the center of the room, lit up in a soft glow—but not from any lights overhead or on floors or tables. Instead, track lighting in the ceiling spotlighted onto paintings on the walls.

My almost gasp was caused by seeing that all of the paintings were male nudes—or, more precisely, male torsos. An impossibly muscled—almost cartoonish in its muscle definition—highly erotic torso and legs, bringing to mind that of a muscle-bound satyr.

"Sit on couch. You want drink?"

"Umm, yes," I answered. "A beer is fine, if you have it."

"Bottle or can?"

"A Bottle's fine, thanks."

He laughed. "You choose wisely. But, then again, maybe not."

On that strange note, he left the room and went into another one overlooking the terrace, which looked like it was a bar.

When he came back, he was swinging four bottles of beer—two in each hand—but I hardly noticed them, as shocked as I was.

He was naked. And what immediately dawned on me was that he obviously was the model for the paintings lit up on the walls. And the paintings no longer looked like exaggeration. His body was horrible and magnificent all in one sweeping impression. All of the muscles were where they should be, but they were almost grotesquely overbuilt. His waist was thick, but with plates of muscle rather than fat—his abs looked like those of a Roman breastplate. His chest muscles overpowered his torso so that his waist looked tiny in contrast. And his arms were as thick as telephone poles, with bulging muscles.

His cock was as thick as a telephone pole too, with two baseball-sized balls hanging behind it. He was already in full arousal.

I moaned as he set three of the beer bottles down and, sitting down close beside me, took a big swallow from the bottle still in his hand. Then, encasing me in one arm, he pulled me to him and took my mouth in his.

I almost gagged as the beer swished into my mouth, and then I did gag as his tongue followed.

I closed my eyes, not able to look at his piggish face, and let him hold my mouth captive with his as his hands moved across my body, unbuttoning, unzipping, pulling clothes off my arms and legs.

I was trapped in the embrace of one of his arms while the hand of the other encased my cock and he started a slow pump.

My nerves were standing on end. His technique of tease in the car leading directly into this no-preliminary assault had me on edge and confused. It would have been useless to resist him anyway, but I was completely disarmed, yielding to him. The reflex was involuntary, but my hips were going with the motion of his hand on my cock. He loosened the grip, while keeping my cock encased, and I found myself slow-fucking his fist.

He released my mouth and then, thankfully, all I could see of his head was the bald top, as his mouth was going down onto my chest.

The hand on my cock was crushing now and was beginning a faster, more demanding cadence.

My eyes went to the paintings on the wall. His body really was a wonder. And none of the paintings showed his face. I could take the body. I looked back down at him and could see—and appreciate—the bulge of the shoulder and muscles on either side of his shiny, billiard-ball-smooth head. He was pulling me over into his lap, and I could feel his hard cock at the small of my back and those thunderous thighs under my naked ones.

I panted hard to the rhythm of his jacking, and I cried out in little huffs of breath in response to what he was doing with his mouth on my nipples.

I shouldn't just be giving it to him. He was a gross pig. I should let him know I didn't want it—or that I'd give it to him but not because I wanted it. Because I didn't have any other choice. Make him demand it and take it by force and then not be able to fully enjoy it, as I couldn't enjoy sex from a beast like this.

If I just didn't have to . . . look . . . at his face.

I brought my hands up to glide over the lines of his fantastically defined muscles.

It was OK, in the almost dark, with the lights just highlighting the paintings. I could let him have it and enjoy it.

I wanted to reach back and grab his cock—to get the measure of it. Both thrilling and moaning to the thought of it inside me. Had I ever taken something that thick and long? Would I have a sense of triumph when I had?

God, I wanted it. I moaned and involuntarily whined, "Please . . . please."

I heard him laugh, a low, rumbling chuckle. I couldn't be doing this. I couldn't want it. Not from a coarse pig. As if in evidence, he bit my nipple and I cried out and stiffened.

Fight him, fight him, I screamed inside to myself. Stay stiff. Make him take it. Don't let him know . . . God, I wanted it. I relaxed, all of my senses going to the rising seed in my cock. My butt twitching. My channel crying out for attention.

Fuck me, fuck me, fuck me. I was surprised that I wasn't saying it—that I was only thinking it. It was the fear of the size of him, though—and the fear of having to look into his piggish face while he plowed me that held back what my aroused body wanted me to cry out to him.

That cock. How much of it could I take? Oh, god, give me that cock. Once more I tried reaching around him for it—but his waist was just too thick.

"Come for me," he said in a low, guttural voice. "Come for me."

I realized that I was on the brink of doing just that. And, shockingly I was overcome with a sense of loss and disappointment. No, fuck me, fuck me, fuck me, my mind was screaming.

And then I came for him.

He laughed and released me. He pushed me over to the side, and I just toppled over on my side on the curving sofa.

He stood over me, in magnificent erection. If my eyes just rose up his body as far as his nipples, I could remain in full arousal myself. I knew I could. Just don't look into the face.

He picked one of the beer bottles up from the coffee table set a couple of feet in front of the sofa and handed it to me.

"Drink," he said. "Drink. Then we fuck. No, I fuck; you scream."

He laughed at his little joke. I shuddered. A few seconds before—before I'd exploded—I'd wanted the cock. Not now. Now I was scared of it again. I could see his evil, piggish face again.

He had already finished off one of the other bottles. I took the bottle, keeping my eyes at the level of his navel, although they kept moving down to his cock and balls and causing little shivers to go up my spine.

I took several swigs, and so did he.

But then he took the bottle from me and put it back on the coffee table.

He turned and sat on the sofa, ran an arm under me, lifted me up, and pulled me over to his lap, facing him. I turned my eyes to one of the paintings on the wall.

Here we go, I said to myself. Remember not to hold your breath. Breathe easily, don't tense your channel, be loose, very loose. Eyes on the paintings. It's the body. You're being taken by that magnificent body. That monstrous cock. Not the face.

But then, rather than setting me down on his cock, he pushed my head toward the carpet in front of the sofa. I felt his thighs go over mine on each side as my shoulders and neck hit the carpet. My thighs were trapped between his and the edge of the sofa. My legs were spread in the air. His feet were on my shoulders at the arm pits, holding my shoulders to the floor.

I shuddered as I saw his face above mine and then, again, when he reached over and took the fourth bottle of beer from the coffee table.

I lurched and gasped and he laughed as I felt the cold beer stream into my channel. And then the neck of the beer bottle.

"Good choice, maybe, the bottle not the can. But when I fuck you, you will wish you had been prepared by the can."

I whimpered and moaned as he fucked me with the neck of the beer bottle, my channel sloshing with beer.

He took my dick in both hands and started to work it again. "You come for me."

I was overcome for several moments, but then I got angry. No, you come for me god dammit. Fuck me. Fuck me.

Again it was an internal cry.

But I managed to reach up with both of my hands and grasp his cock and start driving him as hard as he was driving me.

He let out an animalistic yell, and the first thing I knew, I was dangling from his side with his arm around my waist and we were moving across the room.

Into another room we went, dark, but for only a brief moment. When the lights went on, it was another room with lighting spotting on paintings. Three of them. The same grotesquely gorgeous torso. But fucking a small, dark-skinned youth—a Thai I presumed—in three different positions.

It was a bedroom, with a gigantic king-sized bed in the center of it.

I was dumped on the bed, on my belly. The hand under me, palming my waist, pulled me up onto my knees, while the fist of Jaguerman's other hand grabbed me by the back of my neck and smashed my face into the thick material of the bedspread.

I managed to turn my head and found myself facing a painting of just this fuck position. The cock of the top in the painting was gigantic.

I cried out as Jaguerman's cock head fought for entry in my channel. But only with the bulb of the cock. Pressing in but holding there.

Again the tease, the hint of preliminaries as briefly the bulb moved back and forth just inside my entrance—and then the long plunge, with no further preliminaries.

Yes, fuck me, fuck me. Don't hold your breath, reach back and pull your buttocks apart, relax, relax, relax your channel, relax your . . . oh god, oh GOD. Oh, Holy SHIT! Oh, yesss!

Fuck me, fuck me, fuuccckk me. Moooannn.

Oh, shit, I've got it all. Can feel his pubes on my buttocks. Breathe, breathe. Oh, holy shit. But I've done it. I could do it.

And then, as I felt his balls begin to slap on the tender skin of my inner thighs, the screaming started. It was mine. Giving me no quarter, he was pistoning me to beat the band.

The second painting had me lapped, facing away from him and making love to his cock with my channel. Slower, more sensuous this time. Lovers finding each other's arousal points.

Now he had lost control too. Now he was moaning and groaning.

And it was OK. No, it was great—as long as I wasn't facing him.

But in the third painting position, I was facing him. Laying on my back on the bed, with him standing between my legs.

But I was beyond caring what he looked like. Every fiber of my senses was concentrated on the gigantic staff inside me. Deeper, deeper, thicker. Moan. Faster, deeper, deeper. Oh god, oh shit!

He didn't come. I came. He said, "You come for me," and I came. But then he stopped.

I looked up into his face. Just barely being able to do so now. Any man who could fuck me like that deserved to be looked in the face.

With him stopped, inside me, like that, I could get the measure of him as never before. No, I'd never had it like that before. Never as deep, never as thick. And it was pulsating inside me.

I was mewing and sighing and groaning. "Fuck me, fuck me. Don't stop."

It wasn't spoken internally now. I'd said it. I looked him in his piggish face and I was all desire, no disgust.

"Fuck me," I whined. "Finish it. And then fuck me again."

He was smiling. It was an evil, mischievous smile.

He held there, inside me. I half expected a sudden flow, a gut-wrenching drenching to rival that of the beer.

But he was withdrawing from me. And I wanted to cry. I clutched for his buttocks, trying to hold him inside me.

But he laughed and pushed my hands aside.

I was exhausted. I had just realized that. When he was inside me, everything had been focused on that monster shaft and begging it to reach further, to stretch wider. To throb and to flood me.

But now that was gone, I felt the loss of it. I whimpered.

He laughed. And then he reached down for me and lifted me off the bed and slung me over his shoulder.

He padded across the room and out into the hall. Down the hall to another closed door. He opened the door to darkness. He flipped on the light switch.

Again, spotlights on paintings on three walls, the fourth wall a solid sheet of glass overlooking the terrace and the sultry Bangkok night, the noise of a city that never slept spiraling up into the room.

I whimpered again as my eyes focused on the paintings. Three men now. One of them my Belgian satyr. The other another burly Westerner. Again a small Oriental youth between them. Three fuck positions. All doubles. Two cocks, fighting for dominance, within the small youth's channel.

On the bed, waiting for us. Naked and in full erection. Kamrod Tikka. Smiling. Hand encasing erect phallus.

"There," the Belgian boomed out, "I told you Mr. Tikka would meet us at the apartment."

"Oh god, oh god," I murmured. Not able to respond in any other way in my utter exhaustion.

As Kamrod held his rod stiff and licked his lips in anticipation, the Belgian turned me away from Kamrod and lowered my channel on his cock.

Kamrod encircled my waist with his arms and took my cock in one of his fists. He kissed me in the hollow of my neck.

I watched Jaguerman full in the face as he fisted my ankles, spread my legs up and wide, and began working his cock inside my channel above Kamrod's already fully encased staff.

"Oh, god, oh, god, Oh shit." But it was barely a whimper.

# DREAMWORLD

It's not that Sean didn't see and understand the effect he had on other men; it's just that since he entered his dreamworld with jacko242 he didn't really give a shit. And it wasn't as if he hadn't been a player before he had succumbed to his new world.

His boss in the architectural firm had known Sean would put out—and he certainly had no inkling why Sean still wasn't putting out. There was that corner office on the second floor he'd been grooming Sean for—and that he'd been holding over Sean's head to get every ounce of tail out of his young and winsome employee that he could get. Phil Ocksen thought of Sean as his last fling, a delicious confection he could poke at will. Phil wasn't exactly decrepit yet, but he was moving along in age. He was doing all of the right things in diet and exercise and grooming, and, yes, although he wouldn't admit it, a bit of a nip and tuck here and there.

He was just as presentable, however, as the day he trapped Sean in the filing room and almost blatantly asked Sean what he would do to get that raise he wanted. This had led, just as he'd hoped it would, to fucking Sean on the Xerox machine—with the machine scanning and flipping out images of Sean's flattened buttocks and spread thighs and the underside Phil's very nice cock as it buried itself in Sean's ass and reappeared only to bury itself again. Far from being ashamed of his cock and balls—which had never seen the edge of a plastic surgeon's knife, he wanted to make quite clear—Phil had saved the Xeroxes and still took them out now and again to reminisce about the day he conquered that particular conquest.

But Phil didn't know about jacko242. So that afternoon when he was leaning over Sean to look at some blueprints on Sean's drafting table and was murmuring about how the light was so much better to view these blueprints in that now-empty corner office on the second floor *and* was unbuttoning a button on Sean's sports shirt and running his fingers in to find a nipple hiding in the soft blond down on Sean's chest, Phil had no idea why Sean wasn't reacting as he wished. Sean was being polite and attentive, but he was making no effort whatsoever to warm up to Phil's signaling. Only four weeks earlier this nipple play would have had Sean on his back on the floor, reaching up to Phil's belt buckle as Phil knelt between Sean's spread legs, and pulling Phil's cock inside him while sighing sweet nothings about "big daddy."

Sean wanted that corner office—and he sure as hell wanted the subsidy Phil gave him for the house on Queensbury Row—so Phil assumed that there was some pale of desirability and acceptability that he himself had passed beyond that made him less attractive to Sean. He checked himself in the mirror on the way back to the office. Yep, same forgivingly matured face and full head of hair with distinguished graying at the temples. Same straight back and flat stomach. He reached his hand down. Yep, the same nice cock dressed left in his tailored slacks. But were those crows' feet at the corners of his eyes? Surely that couldn't have been enough for Sean to spurn him. Still, he'd have his secretary, Mavis, call his plastic surgeon.

Sean left the office that afternoon, not even fully aware that he had cut off an advance by Phil. He wasn't thinking of Phil at all. His mind was in that small room at the end of the corridor on the second floor of his house. The one he padded to naked, on bare feet, at night when the house was dark and silent other than the soft snoring of Rod.

He almost absentmindedly entered the backseat of the Lincoln Town Car. Phil had thoughtfully provided this service to take the senior staff members into the exclusive old section of the city where parking was at such a premium and life was so self-contained that many did not have cars and those who did preferred not to take them out of whatever premium parking space they had finally scored.

Phil had instituted the car service two years previously, and Julio had served as the executives' chauffeur from day one. Julio liked the job. The transport hours for the firm's executives worked quite well around his sessions at the gym, where he was training hard to be a champion heavyweight boxer. Other than driving and working out in the gym, Julio had only one vice: cute-looking and saucy blond male tail. Sean had been a hot little number when Julio had come on board, and it hadn't taken long to figure out that the boss, Phil Ocksen, was fucking this nice piece of tail. Julio wanted some of that for himself, and within two weeks of coming on board, Sean had been game for the long ride home and a somewhat shorter but very explosive ride from Julio in the back of the Town Car, with Sean's heels leveraging off the back of the front seat and Julio knelt between Sean's legs and pile driving his puckered ass.

Since that first fucking, Sean had been willing to drop trou and spread legs on just one meaningful look from Julio in the rearview mirror. The cute young blond was a veritable male nympho—a satyriasis. And Julio enjoyed manhandling him and listening to him groan and moan as a dark tan Hispanic monster cock slowly buried itself inside him and Julio started a fast and furious ride that benefited greatly from many hours of thrusting and parrying in the practice boxing ring.

All of this was right up until a couple of weeks ago. And then the arrangement had died cold, very dead, turkey. Julio didn't know what was wrong, but his cock missed the tight warmth of Sean's channel. Maybe Sean was getting that promotion he was always talking about and it just hadn't been announced. Maybe Sean was going up in the world—he certainly had a tight fist on Phil Ocksen's balls, so there was nothing he couldn't ask for in the architectural firm—and maybe Sean was getting uppity. He was a really, really nice piece of ass, and up to recent weeks he'd been so randy for the fucking Julio could give him that he almost begged for it whenever he entered the Town Car. But not now. When Julio gave him "that look" in the rearview mirror, Sean wasn't even looking. His eyes were glazed over, and he was off in some dreamworld somewhere.

Uppity or not, Julio felt like driving into the woods and parking and coming up over the seat back into the backseat and giving Sean the rough fuck of his life. A couple of weeks ago Sean even would have loved that. But not now. Now he was off in a world of his own where Julio was transparent. Julio's cock and balls ached to be fucking the blond little piece of ass. But most of all his pride was aching. An Hispanic fucking the lights out of a little blond Gringo. Now that had been worth talking about down at the gym.

It wasn't anything Sean was holding against Julio specifically or Hispanics in general, though. Julio just didn't know about jacko242.

Sean barely waved an acknowledgment of Julio's good-bye when they arrived in Queensbury Row, and, anger rising inside him, Julio flipped Sean off—but well below the window sill of the Town Car, as Julio wanted to keep his cushy job—and pulled the Lincoln away from the curb and into traffic a bit faster than was really warranted.

Hearing the squeal of the tires, the occupant of the townhouse next door to Sean's, one Professor Steven Connolly, paused at the door while rummaging around in his mailbox and cast a forlorn eye on Sean ascending absentmindedly to his own front door. Steven almost called out something to Sean. But then he stopped, sad, in resignation, and stepped back into the shadows of his foyer.

That phase of Professor Connolly's life was closed now. And although the professor didn't know why it had been cut off so abruptly and so definitively, not more than a month earlier, he could recognize "the end" to an affair as well, if not better than most. Sean had been such an open and fun-loving young man. When Connolly's long-term companion had died, Sean had been so sympathetic and understanding and had provided just the medicine the grieving professor had needed. He had pulled Connolly out of his blue funk one gloomy afternoon in the study in his home, when Sean had taken him by the hand and pushed him gently down into his desk chair. He then had knelt in front of Connolly, slowly unzipped his pants, and sucked Connolly's cock to paradise. After that Sean had stripped off his own clothes and sat on Connolly's now-very-hard cock, facing him, and had slowly fucked himself to their mutual completion and satisfaction.

Subsequently, on most workday evenings, Sean had mounted the stairs to Connolly's Queensbury Row townhouse before entering his own when arriving home from work. Connolly had waited for him, trembling, in the foyer, and then the two had ascended the stairs, hand in hand, and in silence moved to the bedroom where, for decades, Connolly and his companion had made love. And just then, for that brief afternoon period, Connolly was transported back to happier times as Sean laid down on his back on the bed and spread his thighs and Connolly sank his cock deep into the younger man's world.

And then, just when Connolly was building up to the suggestion of a more permanent arrangement, Sean had just stopped coming for their late-afternoon assignations. No explanations, no harsh words, no formal ending—just an abrupt, total ending. Now Sean mounted his own stairs when he returned from work, no longer visiting the house next door to be mounted by Professor Connolly. And always that blank expression on Sean's face as if he was totally off in another world.

Steven Connolly had no idea what had changed—but then he knew nothing about jacko242. All Connolly knew was that he had not left his house since Sean's last visit—everything he needed he had had delivered—and that he spent his late afternoons tangled in the sheets of his lost companion's bed, naked, and writhing against the sheets, fucking the sheets, until he had exhausted himself and relieved his grief and loneliness in spent cum and tears.

When Sean entered his Queensbury Row house, his senses were immediately assaulted. There was humming in a deep baritone coming from the kitchen and from there as well the smells of an oregano-laced spaghetti sauce. The combination of the two meant that it was Italian night. It also signaled that Rod was in high heat and wanted to fuck on the bearskin rug in front of the fireplace.

Sean sighed and checked through the mail. All of the time he was doing this, though, and listening to his lover's humming from the kitchen, Sean's mind had already mounted the stairs and walked deliberately down the hall to the small room at the end—and to jacko242. It just wasn't time yet, though. Sean ached for the hours to slip by until the appointed time.

Sighing again, Sean turned and moved toward the kitchen. He knew what he would find, and he was right. Enhanced aromas of the cooking sauce, two glasses of Burgundy on the island top, and a smiling, naked, black-skinned god in full erection. Rodney Singleton had come into Sean's life just a bit more than a year earlier. A star receiver of the metropolitan area's professional football team, he had come to Sean's architectural firm, annual bonus in hand, wanting to build his dream house on the cliffs overlooking the sea in a nearby suburb. At this point Phil Ocksen had made possibly the biggest mistake of his life. He had turned the big black hunk over to Sean for drawing up the concept layouts for the project, and within an hour of their meeting, Sean was bent over the toilet in the small bathroom off his office and Rod was crouched over him from behind, palming Sean's pert little nipples in his big football-receiver's mitts, and giving Sean as deep a doggy fuck as he'd ever had.

Rod moved in with Sean rather than building that house, and Phil lost not only the client but also a good chunk of Sean's sexual favors. Rodney's sexual demands were enough to exhaust a horse.

Rodney was highly sexed and not all that observant, which was probably just fine for his mental well-being. He had barely even noticed that Sean had been somewhere else—in his own dreamworld—for weeks.

When Sean had entered the kitchen and taken a sip of Burgundy with hardly any greeting at all—or any appreciative look at that magnificent cock rising below Rod's washboard belly and bulging, barrel chest—Rodney completely failed to notice Sean's vacant expression when, as he so often did, he murmured. "So glad you're home, baby. I'm so full of cum, I'm about to explode. Strip for me, honey. We have a good hour before the sauce is finished."

Sean absentmindedly stripped down as requested, took another sip of Burgundy, and then docilely followed Rod into the living room, to the bearskin rug, in front of a fire set in the fireplace. He laid down on his back and raised his trim ankles to the shoulders of his magnificent black lover who was kneeling between his thighs. Sean turned his head toward the mesmerizing fire and let his mind wander to that little room on the second floor and to jacko242, as, with a grunt, Rod entered him strongly with his throbbing cock and dragged that thick silver cock ring along Sean's channel, deep inside him. Sean raised his hips and let them slowly drift into the familiar undulation of the rhythm of the deep fuck, his body responding, if minimally, but his mind off in its own dreamworld. Rod didn't notice that some part of Sean was missing. He hadn't had a fuck in nearly twelve hours and he needed to get his rocks off. And Sean had the sweetest passage in town. Rodney just grunted and thrust away, coming in great gobs of milky-white jism, deep inside Sean's sweet hole, just as the timer was going off for the bubbling tomato sauce.

Rodney was equally unobservant that night, when, balls once more aching for sex, he trapped Sean's compliant, docile body, belly down on the sheets, under his, gripped Sean's hips close between his knees, and rode his little blond pony hard through two mighty ejaculations. Then spent and satisfied himself, Rod rolled Sean over on his side, cock still buried, still deeply sheath even in flaccidity, and spooned Sean into his chest. Rod went into a deep, satisfied, fulfilled sleep, not needing another fuck for a good eight hours—in the morning he'd take Sean up against the tiles of the shower before Sean left for work and then he'd putter around the townhouse all day—this being his off season—except for a three-hour session in the training room down at the stadium and then be cum filled again and hard for Sean's return from work.

All a good, fulfilling day for Rodney—and especially so since he was blessedly unaware that Sean hadn't really been there, other than providing a compliant hole to poke, for several weeks. Sean had been off in his own dreamworld and in the thrall of jacko242.

Hours later, in the darkest of night, with Rodney snoring contentedly in his ear, Sean slowly and quietly disentangled himself from Rodney's possessive embrace and sat up on the side of the bed. His cock was hard and dripping with precum, and his breath was ragged—in anticipation. He was in heat for the first time today. Neither the advances of the elegant, experienced Phil in the office; nor what most young men would see as the enticement of the delectable Hispanic chauffer, Julio; nor the hopeful—eternally grateful—proffering gaze of Professor Connolly at his door—nor the exuberant attentions of the masterfucker black stud Rodney had set Sean's juices going.

But the thought of that little room down the hall and of jacko242 had done so.

Sean stood up beside the bed, still naked. He ran his hand up from his hard cock along his belly to his nipples and flicked them with his thumb. Already puffed out, hard. He padded out of the room quietly and down the hall and into the small computer room. He shut the door behind him. He knew that he might cry out upon release, and he didn't want to wake Rodney—although a temporarily well-fucked Rodney could sleep through an earthquake.

Sean sat down on the terrycloth covered desk chair and fired up the computer. When he had a browser screen, he tapped in www.mandate.net and then clicked on the profile of jacko242.

There he was, the love of Sean's life, in all of his naked glory. Beautiful, sun-kissed body. Turkish features, a well-muscled hunk with black, curly body hair. Square-cut facial features and that knowing smile. Knowing that Sean had returned to him.

Sean clicked on "live-chat," and he was there, waiting for Sean.

"You're late."

"Sorry. I'm here now. Hard to get away tonight."

"Are you hard?"

"Yes, for you always, Jacko," Sean tapped out. And that was true. He was as hard as he could be.

"Stroke it."

Sean complied.

"Is there precum yet?"

Yes, there certainly was.

"Taste it."

Sean did so. A little moan escaped his lips.

"Look at my cock in the photo. It is for you. Is it big enough for you? And thick enough?"

"Yes, oh yes."

"Close your eyes. Run your hands up my belly and into my chest hair. Feel my nipples? Hard for you."

"Yes, oh yes," Sean replied. He was leaning back in his chair, running hands up to his own nipples. As hard as he imagined Jacko's to be.

"Do you have the cock? Is it lubed?"

"Yes and yes," Sean tapped out. He reached for the dildo he had lubed up while the computer was warming up.

"Close your eyes. Work it in. It's my cock. Inside you. Making love to your walls."

For the next couple of minutes, while the computer screen murmured words of instruction and lovemaking, Sean moaned and groaned in ecstasy. His thighs were spread and hooked over the arms of his desk chair, his hips rolled forward on the front edge of the chair and one hand stroking his cock and the other working the dildo deep in his passage . . . as the honeyed phrasing of the words on the screen fucked him masterfully.

As long last, at the height of a passion that Sean had felt at no earlier point of his day, Sean gave a little cry and jerked several times as he ejaculated into the hand cloth he held over his cock head.

He looked up. The screen was blank. Jacko242 had left him. But jacko242 had left him feeling deeply touched to the very quick of him—once again. Sean would somehow have to endure through another day. Jacko242 was only there for him for this one hour of the night. Sean had no idea whether he could wait for his next deeply satisfying encounter with his jacko242.

\* \* \* \*

At a dingy workbench in the back of a double garage in suburban Jefferson City, smack dab in the middle of the flattest, most monotonous Midwestern U.S. state, Elmer Dent had quickly switched from one profile on Mandate.net to the next. It had been a touch-and-go thing. Piningblond had been late this evening—again, for the second time this week. Jacko242 thought perhaps he'd have to cut him off; he wasn't fitting into the schedule well. He flipped over to Legsopen4u, who was already there, on time, as usual.

"Are you hard?" Elmer tapped out under his jacko242 name. He ran his hand inside his robe and scratched his belly, not even bothering to look at the response from legsopen4u before tapping in the next sequence. "Stroke it." The response was always the same—as were his instructions. These computer sex junkies never seemed to notice the sameness of it all. Elmer took a swig of his beer and burped.

A faint sound, coming through several of the thin walls in the squat tract rancher. "Elmer. You out in the garage again? Come to bed and do me, hon. Turn off that computer."

Elmer sighed. That Hazel was so demanding. If she weren't the one with the job—down at the Laundromat . . .

"Just a minute, sweet cheeks," Elmer called back, pulling his robe closer together over his paunch and reaching down and scratching his hairy balls. "Just about done out here."

And he was, in fact, just about done. Legsopen4u was his last computer sex junkie of the evening. While he'd waited for piningblond to click on, he'd browsed the new members. There was a nice-sounding profile obviously just aching for it who he might like to ride for a while. Maybe he'd give him piningblond's slot. That one was about to play out anyway. It had been four weeks.

~

# About the Author

**Habu** is one of the pen names of a former supersonic spy jet pilot, intelligence agent, male model, movie actor, and diplomat. A wild youth in South East Asia was spent enjoying whatever sexual opportunities came his way, and much of his gay male writing is about recalling incidents from those days and inventing ones he'd perhaps have liked to experience. He now leads a very quiet and ordinary happily married family life.

An American, he is a published mainstream novelist and short story writer under another name and in another dimension of his life. He has written or cowritten (with Sabb) approaching 1,000 published short stories and over 100 published erotica e-books, primarily of gay fiction but also memoir, straight fiction and ménage fiction. His hand and creative writing can be seen in stories and books by habu, sr71plt, Dirk Hessian, Shabbu, and Stephen Kessel—among unrevealed others that might surprise readers. The fictionalized GM memoir *Flying High, Diving Deep* is loosely based on his life experiences. He can be found at the adults only gay male site www.BarbarianSpy.com, which he shares with Sabb, Dirk Hessian, and Alex Lockheed.

Our authors always like to receive feedback, and appreciate it when readers post reviews at distributors and other sites.

# BarbarianSpy
## FOR LITERARY HEAT

**Not all books listed below may currently be on release.**
\* indicates the book is available in paperback and e-book.

## BOOKS BY ALEX LOCKHEED
### Transsexual Romance
Meeting Jenna
Being Sarah

## BOOKS BY DIRK HESSIAN
### Xtreme Erotica
The King's Men
Shores of Tripoli
Prophecy of Noto
Pretender's Fate
### General Erotica/Romance
Fire Down the Valley\*
Constantinople\*
The Beautiful Way\*
Blue and Gray
Colonel's Treasure
Beginning of Time
Labyrinth

## BOOKS BY HABU
### Gay Erotica
### Memoir Faction
Flying High, Diving Deep\*
### Xtreme Erotica
Silas' Choice\*
Last Call
Choke Hold
Apyko: The Greek Pimp
Visits of the Schlange
Second Coming: Emile La Cour Unleashed
Vortex: Sacrificed by Curiosity\*

Dark Angel Sounding *(in e-book & included in Sounding:Ultimate Control Paperback)**
Sounding: Ultimate Control (*Print Only*)*
Sounding Five *(in e-book & included in Sounding:Ultimate Control paperback)**

## Romance
Tank n Bull
Sail to the Sun
War Letters
Ravens Roost
Caribbean Cruise Top to Bottom
Arena Stage
Trading Partners (Valentine's Day)
Friday Nights with Lenny (Christmas Romance)
Snowy, Snowy Nights (Christmas Romance)
Four Coins
Lower Than the Heart (Valentine's Day)
Brambleton
Gotta Keep Trying
Finding Amnad
Platres Conclave

## Other Novels/Novellas
Journey Through Abilene
Harmony and Dissonance
Stallion Station
Racing With the Devil (espionage suspense)
Cruising Gigolo (bisexual)
Prepared in Cape Verdi
Gilded Cage
House on Park
Anything for Ambition
Dance of the Ravishers
Hard Knocks U*
My Neighbor's Spa*
Man's Man: Tales of a High Priced Gay Hooker*
Trip Money
The Indian Doctor

Sailorboy
Home to Fire Island
**Murder Mysteries**
Death on a Ping Pong Table
Clint Folsom Mysteries Compendium Volume 1*
Death to Blonds - Stolen Judgment (Clint Folsom Mystery)*
Clint Folsom Mysteries Compendium Volume 2*
**Gay Erotica Anthologies**
Eight in D
DevilMENt
Silas' Choices*
Stallion Station (A Novella in Parts)
Eleven to the Dogs*
Fifty Seventy*
Spy Tails 001*
Spy Tails 002*
Doubled*
Doubled Again*
Tails in the Tropics*
Tails in the Med*
Tails in the West*
Rough Riders*
Grab Bag 1*
Grab Bag 2*
Grab Bag 3*
Grab Bag 4*
Grab Bag 5*
Grab Bag 6*
Beyond the Beaded Curtain*
Habu's Christmas Balls
The Sporting Life*
Fetish Galore!*
**Literary Gay Erotica**
Cairo Surrender*
The Handyman*
Homeward Bound

Journey to Mirage*
**Bi-Sexual/Menage Erotica**
Death on a Ping Pong Table
Cruising Gigolo
13 Ways for Halloween
Luther*
The Indian Prince
**Literary GLBT Fiction**
Summer of Denial
**BOOKS BY SABB**
Hiring in Hollywood
The Legend of Holleystone Grange
Surprise Encounters
She is He
Wrong Man
Loyal to his King
Barbarian Tales - Book One - Traveler's Tales*
Barbarian Tales - Book Two - Journeys Begin*
Barbarian Tales - Book Three - The Inheritance*
Barbarian Tales - Book Four - Road to Persepolis*
**BOOKS BY SHABBU**
Velvet Interrogation
Finding Jason
Dirty Pool
Operation Black Jade
Cigars!*
Angel in the Barn
Gayly Complicated*
Despoiling David
The Tree of Idleness*
I Met a Man
Rough Road to Happiness
**BOOKS BY STEPHEN KESSEL**
**Gay Romance**
The Forever Man*
Two Chances

www.ingramcontent.com/pod-product-compliance
Lightning Source LLC
Chambersburg PA
CBHW021923170626
46807CB00007B/2958